TEXAS FRIDAYS

ODESSA

SAM MOUSSAVI

EPIC
Press

Odessa
Texas Fridays

Written by Sam Moussavi

Published by EPIC Press™
PO Box 398166
Minneapolis, MN 55439

Cover design by Kali Yeado
Images for cover art obtained from iStockPhoto.com
Edited by Gil Conrad

LIBRARY OF CONGRESS CATALOGING-IN-PUBLICATION DATA

Names: Moussavi, Sam, author.
Title: Odessa / by Sam Moussavi.
Description: Minneapolis, MN : EPIC Press, 2017. | Series: Texas Fridays
Summary: Private detective Pete Hamilton is called upon to investigate the disappearance of
    a female student at Permian High School named Winona Daughtry. Before disappearing,
    Winona was known to be in a relationship with one of Permian's star players on the varsity
    football team, Les Myers.
Identifiers: LCCN 2016946211 | ISBN 9781680764956 (lib. bdg.) |
    ISBN 9781680765519 (ebook)
Subjects: LCSH: High school—Fiction. | Football—Fiction. | Football players— Fiction. |
    Missing persons—Fiction. | Life change events—Fiction. | Young adult fiction.
Classification: DDC [Fic]—dc23
LC record available at http://lccn.loc.gov/2016946211

EPIC
Press

EPICPRESS.COM

For those eager to take liberties with the imagination and stay awhile.
—Pete Simonelli

1

IT WAS MID-SEPTEMBER WHEN I GOT THE CALL FROM Winona's parents. Their teenage daughter had been missing a week by then, which was not unusual for her, necessarily. She had run away before. Winona Daughtry was a senior at Permian High School in Odessa. I was hired to find her. According to her parents, sometime before disappearing, she'd had a relationship with a boy at school named Les Myers. Les was a god-like figure at Permian—the best middle linebacker Odessa had seen since Bront Bird in the early 2000s.

I started with Les because that's always the place

you start—with the boyfriend. I parked my car in Permian's student lot on Monday, September twenty-fifth, a cloudy day that threatened a rain that never came.

"Hello, I'm here to see Coach Freeman," I said to the little lady behind the desk in Permian's admin office.

"Have an appointment?"

"Athletic director said Coach Freeman could give me a few minutes around lunch."

"Ain't time for lunch yet," she said, thrusting her chin back at the mounted clock on the wall behind her. "Still in fourth period."

"I'll wait."

"Park yourself over there."

The stout little moon-faced lady went back to her work, and I sat in an empty chair across from her. The bell that ended fourth period rang fifteen minutes later, and after the students flooded the halls and got to the next place they needed to be, I shot the little lady a look. She picked up the phone at her desk and mumbled into the receiver. Then she hung up the phone and regarded me acerbically.

"He'll see you now," she said. "Out the hallway, two rights and then a left."

I tipped my hat to her after standing up. She didn't care too much for me. I understood that I had crossed a line simply by being there.

The halls were covered with banners, and as I made the first right, there was a long trophy case—longer than the one in the front lobby of the school. The case was filled with gold trophies, old jerseys, and photographs from Permian Panthers' teams of the past. There was no memory of Les Myers's Permian football career anywhere in the case, but perhaps his story was still being written. As for Winona Daughtry, the clock was ticking down to zero to find her. Nobody was racing to commemorate her achievements and place them behind glass—that much was clear.

Coach Freeman's office was right where the little lady said it would be. I guess I expected that she'd send me to the boiler room before sending me where I really wanted to go. But there I was. I took a deep breath before knocking on the sturdy door. I knew that this thing I was working on was not going to be simple.

I knocked twice, loudly.

"Come in," a burly voice said from inside.

I walked inside, and there was Coach Freeman behind his desk. He was a large man, but not fat, and his eyes were lively, although almost entirely caged by the sockets. The office smelled like coffee and tobacco. Coach Freeman wore a black, short-sleeved golf shirt with the Permian Panthers' logo over his heart. Underneath the logo—a screaming Panther head—were the words "Permian Pride," and underneath that, "MOJO," the school's famous rallying cry for all things pigskin.

"Coach Freeman," I said, extending my hand.

He hesitated before reaching out and giving me his huge right hand. His right forearm bulged with tension as we shook. The room was sticky-hot with no air-conditioning. That struck me as odd, as Permian never lacked for funding, especially the football program. Then I got a real good look at Coach Freeman, and it became clear. He was the sort of man who thrived in discomfort. The kind of man who turned up the heat just to be hot. The pressure of big-time Texas high school football had hardened him against the elements—both inside and out. Or maybe I had it backwards, and he was one of those who took the struggles of life in stride.

I took off my hat and sat down in front of him, wiping my forehead with my sleeve.

"Is it hot in here?" he asked.

"A bit," I replied.

"Oh hell," he said. "I guess I didn't even notice. I get so wrapped up in what we got going on."

"It's fine."

"Want me to turn the AC on?"

"It's really okay."

"What can I do for you, Mr . . . ?"

"Hamilton. Pete Hamilton," I said. "Please call me Pete."

"Okay, Pete."

"I spoke to your athletic director late last week. It was regarding the disappearance of Winona Daughtry."

"Yes, Russ told me about his talk with you."

"He said you would give me a few minutes to answer any questions I had."

Coach Freeman's brow furrowed involuntarily. "Yes?" he said.

We sat there staring at each other for a short time. He watched me blankly, though his eyes maintained their intensity. There wasn't any hate in his eyes. Not yet anyway. But he wasn't going to go out of his way to help me either.

"What do you do, Pete?" he asked finally.

"Huh?" I said, startled that he spoke first. "What do you mean?"

"I mean, what do you do? You see, I coach

football. Pretty straightforward, no? I'm trying to understand what it *is* that you do."

"I've been hired to find Winona."

"And is Winona here?"

"No."

"Then what are you doing in my office asking me about Winona Daughtry? You should be out there looking for her." He held a rigid pointer finger past my head and out into the world.

I opened my mouth to reply but stopped when I saw a rapturous smile curling onto his face.

"I'm only kidding, Pete. I'm happy to help. But I don't know why the hell Russ told you that I'd answer all of your questions," he said. "Can't imagine what answers he or you think I have. But I'll take that up with Russ later."

His face was calm and the curious smile remained.

"I'm planning to talk to Les Myers," I said, giving him a dose of my own fortitude. "I'm here first to ask your permission because it's the decent thing to do. I don't know if you were aware that

Les and Winona were seeing each other before she disappeared."

He stood up and gave me a look at his entire frame. Looming over me, Coach Freeman looked like he could still get out there and play. I could picture how this stance would scare the Holy Ghost out of high school kids. But to me, his intention was not overtly antagonistic. The weird smile was still there on his face, but I was relaxed and in no fear of impending danger.

"They stopped seeing each other before that," he said. Then he closed his eyes in disgust. He'd stepped in it and knew it. He had said too much.

"What's that?" I asked.

His eyes stayed glued on mine. "You need to leave, Mr. Hamilton."

"Call me Pete."

"Please, Pete," he said, shaking his head. "You need to go. Les has nothing to tell you. When she, Winona, first disappeared, I was there when the cops talked to Les. They cleared him of any foul play right then."

"Who interviewed Les?"

"A detective from the OPD."

"Do you remember his name?" I asked.

"No," he replied. "If there were any way I could help you, I would. But I don't know anything. And as for Les, this is a big year for him. I don't want any other distractions for him or the rest of the squad."

"Okay," I said, standing up.

"Oh and I'd appreciate it, Pete, if you didn't try to talk to any of my other boys either."

I put on my hat.

"Thank you for your time, Coach."

I extended my hand and he clutched it weakly. He knew he had said too much.

2

I LEFT PERMIAN AND WENT BACK TO MY OFFICE TO take care of a few things. I had my first piece of information. Up until that point, I was led to believe that Les and Winona were seeing each other all the way up until Winona's disappearance. Coach Freeman let it slip that there was some time and distance between their association and her being gone. When I put in a call to Les's house to talk to his folks, there was no answer. I knew the chances of them talking to me were slim, but I figured I'd give it a try anyway. At three o'clock, I went back to Permian High for football practice. I parked away from the school this time, in case I needed to exit posthaste. I took a spot high up in the bleachers of Ratliff Stadium to get a good look at the field.

The players came out of the locker room in small groups, and Les came out with one of the last ones wearing number fifty. From up high, I could see the sureness in his step. This confidence was likely written on his face as well, but I hadn't had the chance to test this theory out yet. I knew from word around town—not to mention the paper—that Les could play. He had his pick of three Division I scholarship offers, and at least one other dark-horse school from the south hoped to swoop in and grab him.

The stands were empty during the early week practice, so no one bothered me as the players began stretching. I kept my eye on Les as he loosened up and chatted with teammates and coaches. He had no clue he was being watched. From up there, he looked like any other carefree teenager. There was nothing in his body language that said there was something nasty hanging over him. He joked around with teammates, and when it was time to get serious—like when Coach Freeman stomped onto the field with the rest of his staff—Les did that too. Either the young man was a pro at separating things in his mind, or he was truly innocent.

In my mind, Les Myers was a clear suspect.

Coach Freeman rallied the team around him, and it was then that I understood how big—physically, that is—a team Permian actually was. Coach Freeman was a large man, and at least half the team was just as imposing. I couldn't hear what Coach Freeman was telling his guys, but I could see that he commanded their respect.

The players were standing up straight, their eyes glued ahead. Les was right next to Coach Freeman. There didn't seem to be any laziness or aloofness bred into Les because of his stardom. Coach Freeman broke the circle and sent the players to their individual position drills.

Now, I'm not crazy about high school football

like everyone else down here in Texas—the results of the games make no difference in my day-to-day life. I do know the game, however, and everything that surrounds it. I played in high school down in Fort Stockton—where I'm from—and as a junior, received an All-County honorable mention as a safety. I quit playing for good on the eve of my senior season after some off-the-field issues—both in my parents' home and at school—derailed my focus in the classroom and on the field.

Les and the rest of the linebackers ran through some form-tackling drills. I could tell that number fifty was quick just from watching him in these simple drills. Les was also smart. He never made a false step—the worst sin for a linebacker—when searching for the ball. He simply located the ball and attacked it. As I watched him work, I started thinking about how I was going to make my approach after practice was finished. Then I noticed someone in my periphery walking up the bleachers toward me. When the person came close, I realized that it was just a kid, one of the endless legions of team helpers. The kid came cautiously close until he was right next to me.

"Yeah?" I asked.

"I got a message for you from Coach Freeman."

"What's that?"

The kid took a handwritten note out of his shorts. He cleared his throat and looked at me.

"He says that he asked you nicely earlier—"

"Just get to it," I said.

He looked back down to the note. "He says you have to leave. Practice is closed to the public."

"I didn't even see him turn around to look at me."

"Coach Freeman knows everything." And with that, the water-boy folded the slip of paper and shambled back down the bleachers.

Coach Freeman finally turned around and looked up at me. We locked eyes even with the distance between us. He knew right then that he was going to have trouble getting rid of me. I knew that I had his full attention.

I decided to leave Ratliff Stadium because it was pretty clear I wouldn't be able to get to Les that way. I would have to figure out another way. It was okay though. I wasn't learning anything earth-shattering from watching Les practice. Like I said, I already knew he could play. I was just looking for a sign.

. . . .

I left Permian to go meet with Winona's parents. They lived off Lyndale Drive in a one-story rancher. It was a quiet, working-class neighborhood. Winona's father, Rick, worked as a mechanic, and her mother, Florence, was a seamstress over at a custom tailor shop in town. I didn't know the Daughtrys personally, but an old friend of mine from back in Fort Stockton was Winona's godfather. That old friend referred me to the Daughtrys after the cops in Odessa failed to make any headway on

Winona's whereabouts. When I first spoke to the Daughtrys on the phone, they'd both explained that they worked a lot and that was part of the reason Winona was lost to them in many ways.

I knocked on the Daughtrys' door and waited for a response. Heavy footsteps approached and the door opened. Rick stood there in his oil-stained jumpsuit. He had an open can of Bud in one hand and a cigarette in the other.

"Mr. Daughtry," I said. "I'm Pete Hamilton. We spoke on the phone yesterday."

Rick invited me inside with his eyes although he said nothing. He turned his back to lead the way, and I followed him in. The house had a prominent, lived-in smell. The residence was dark, either by nature or choice, and didn't look like a place for a child, certainly not a happy teenage girl. Rick walked through the living room, on through the kitchen, and finally out onto the patio. Florence was there sitting at a table with a glass of white wine and a cigarette of her own. As expected, there was more emotion in her eyes when she saw me.

"Mr. Hamilton," Florence said, almost startled. "Please sit down."

I took off my hat and sat adjacent to Florence. She was at the head of the table, and Rick was across from me.

"Please, Mrs. Daughtry, call me Pete."

"Call me Florence," she replied.

"Okay."

"Can we offer you something to drink?"

"No, thank you."

"Do you mind our smoking?"

"It's fine."

"You have to ask these days," she said. "When we were younger, everybody smoked. Now . . . " Florence stopped herself and realized her words were unimportant, small talk.

Rick's eyes did not change as his wife observed her hands nervously.

"I went to see Coach Freeman earlier today," I said. "I just left Permian's practice."

"And?" Rick finally said, as if the mention of Permian itself and not his missing daughter was what was of importance to him.

"Nothing much," I said. "Coach Freeman asked me to lay off Les Myers and said that he has been cleared in Winona's investigation."

Rick took a healthy sip of beer and huffed. "And that has you yellow?"

"That's not what I'm saying. I just have to go about talking with Les in a different way."

Florence's eyes held a perpetual shininess around their edges. There was a worn-down quality to her, like there wasn't much fight left. Rick on the other hand, stared at me with steely, hop-soaked eyes. He looked like he was always ready for a fight, and that made me rethink whether or not Winona had been kidnapped. Maybe she was running from something else.

"Coach Freeman did let something slip though, right before I left his office," I said.

A glimmer of hope flashed into Florence's eyes.

"He mentioned that Les and Winona broke it off sometime before she disappeared. That was news to me, according to what you guys told me over the phone yesterday."

Florence and Rick glanced at one another.

"I don't understand," Florence said. "What does it matter when they stopped seeing each other?"

"It matters because Coach Freeman knew he screwed up when he told me that," I said. "You see, he didn't mean to tell me that. It slipped out. And now I have something to go on—evidence that something's not quite right."

"Are you saying that Coach Freeman is involved with Winona's disappearance in some way?" Florence asked.

The Daughtrys watched me as I chewed the question over.

I sighed. "In my business, things need to be off in

order for me to do my job," I said. "It's unfortunate that it has to be that way, but it just is. That's all I'm saying."

"Are you saying that our daughter is dead?" Rick belted out.

"No. I'm not saying that. I'm just saying that Coach Freeman messed up when he told me that about Les and Winona. Now I have to find out *how* he messed up."

Florence took a sip of her wine, and her hand shook as she placed the glass back down on the table. I felt for her. Even though she probably wasn't the best parent, something told me that she didn't deserve this. My feeling for Florence balanced out my dislike for Rick. I decided that I was going to do this for Florence, not only because her daughter was missing, but also because her husband, Rick, didn't seem to be the nicest man.

"Is there anything you forgot to tell me about Les and Winona?" I asked.

Once again the Daughtrys stared at one another.

"Like I told you on the phone," Florence said, "we're not home much. Rick's gone early in the morning, and I'm right out the door a little after he leaves. We don't see Winona much. We have our problems just like any other family. But this isn't right. To have your daughter just up and leave for a week without calling."

Her eyes watered again, and Rick stared straight past me as his wife began to weep. I glared at him, and it took all I had to stop me from telling him to put his hand on his wife's shoulder or comfort her in some way. But I didn't do it.

"You know everything, Mr. Hamilton," Florence said in between sobs.

"Okay," I said, before putting my hat on. "I'm gonna get to Les another way. And talk to Winona's friend, Courtney, in the meantime." I took out a small notepad from my breast pocket.

"Thank you, Mr. Hamilton," she said.

"Call me Pete, please."

Rick finished his beer and cleared his throat. "One more thing," he said.

I turned to him.

"We talked about your fee over the phone last week," he said.

I raised my hand in hopes that he would stop talking. He did.

"Let me get something concrete for you, and then we can talk about payment," I said. "I'll be in touch."

Rick's face held as much gratitude as it possibly could.

"Good evening," I said, as I tipped my hat. "I'll let myself out."

I walked through the Daughtrys' house again, and the dank smell inside gave me a queasy feeling in my gut. As I passed several pictures of the family hanging on the wall, I realized that I hadn't actually *seen* what Winona looked like. Up to that point, I only had Florence's description of her daughter.

I studied each picture as I made my exit. There

were a few of Winona by herself, both as a young child and as a teenager, and there were two pictures with the family all together. She seemed to be an only child because there were no siblings in either of the photos and no mention from her parents of a brother or sister. Winona seemed happy enough in the pictures. I could see no sign that she was anything other than normal. Physically, she was rather tall and thin with long brunette hair. Her eyes were brown, and there was a small mole to the right of her bottom lip.

I stopped in front of the dark hallway that led to the bedrooms. There were two of them. I turned around and walked back to the patio.

Florence and Rick were jarred when I opened the patio door and poked my head out.

"Can I take a look inside Winona's room before I leave?"

Florence put out her cigarette and entered the house, leading me down the dark hallway to the closed door to Winona's room. Before she opened the door, I wished that we'd walk inside to see Winona lying on her bed, doing homework maybe. I wanted this to be over before it started. But I knew better. This was just the beginning.

She opened the door and stepped inside. I followed her, and if you could believe it, the air in Winona's room was even warmer and more putrid than the rest of the house.

"Let me open a window," Florence said, rushing over to the far wall.

There were clothes all over the floor, a pile of wet towels in the corner that partially explained the smell, and two bowls of half-eaten cereal that told the rest. Florence seemed mildly embarrassed but not enough so to pick up the clothes and dishes. I walked to the center of the room and waited there. I scanned the entire room, checking to see if anything jumped out at me. Florence held her breath as if some magic was happening, but really, I just wanted to take it all in. That spot in the middle of the room allowed me to do so. The first object

28

that caught my eye—which is what always catches my eye first—was the dresser.

"Can I open up Winona's dresser drawers, Mrs. Daughtry?"

"Yes."

The wooden dresser had three drawers. I went from the bottom drawer to the top. The bottom two drawers held the various commonplace garments of any person—regardless of age—and there didn't seem to be many clothes gone, kicking dirt on the idea that Winona had planned to skip town for good. I opened the top drawer and rooted through Winona's socks and underwear. This made Florence uncomfortable, so I tried to be quick about it, while also being thorough. There was something solid, pen-like, amongst all that cloth. Something plastic. I pulled it out. It was a home pregnancy test. It was positive. I turned around and held it out to Florence.

"Were you aware that Florence was pregnant?"

She covered her mouth.

No parent wanted to see something like this in their daughter's dresser drawer. But for me, this item would help me do my job. I had direction now.

"I don't believe it," she finally offered.

She took a deep breath and sat down on her daughter's bed. This new revelation placed even more of a burden on this woman's shoulders.

"Did she show any physical signs of being pregnant?" I asked.

"No."

I continued searching the room and there wasn't anything else that you could call peculiar. At the end of my sweep, I found a journal underneath the mattress—its contents usually the portal into a young girl's life. I held up the journal to Florence, who was still sitting on the end of the bed.

"Go ahead," she said. "You've already found the worst."

Not so fast, I thought to myself.

I opened the journal and it was clear that a number of pages had been ripped out.

"Is Winona known to write? Does she like to write?" I asked.

"Isn't it obvious that I don't know anything about my daughter?" she said, venomously. This was the first sign of nastiness that I saw in her.

"I mean, did she write in this journal often?" I asked. "Was she always carrying it around maybe?"

"I've seen her carrying it before," she said, numbly.

I flipped through every page and they were all blank except for the last two. On those final pages were pencil sketches of a man with shoulder-length hair, wearing a white mask. The mask was rounded, giving the effect of a chubby face. But the man was skinny. One of the sketches had the man standing with his arms crossed and the second one had the man sitting on a couch with his right leg across his left.

I sat down next to Florence on the end of the bed.

A beat passed before I handed Winona's journal

to Florence, with it open to the first sketch. She took it and looked at the page closely.

"That doesn't look like Les Myers. Neither in hair length nor body type," I said.

"No," she said.

She flipped to the second sketch with the masked-man sitting.

"What's with the mask?" she asked.

"Does this remind you of anyone in your daughter's life? A friend? Boyfriend?"

She shook her head.

"Did you ever know Winona to be someone who likes to draw? Could this be some kind of character in her head?"

"You probably think that I am the worst mother in the world, but I'm not going to lie to you. I don't know much about Winona. I can't tell you exactly when I started losing my grip on her, but it was somewhere around the beginning of high school."

I avoided her eyes to lessen the pressure. She had enough on her already.

"I don't know if she draws," she said, before starting to cry again.

I put my hand on the back of her shoulder. She cried for a minute or two. After she raised her head, I pointed to Winona's journal, which was in her lap.

"I'm gonna take that with me," I said.

She looked down at the journal and then handed it to me.

"Yeah," she said "Just be careful with it, Mr. Hamilton. That journal seemed to mean something to my daughter. If . . . if she's gone, I'd like to have that back."

"Of course," I said, standing up.

Florence stood up as well.

I leaned in close and lowered my voice.

"About the pregnancy test. It might be best to not say anything to your husband about it. At least until I find some more out."

She nodded and my suggestion seemed to lessen her burden.

"I'll be in touch," I said, before walking out of

the room. I left the Daughtrys' house and walked to my car. The sun was beginning to go down, but the air was thick with humidity. I sat in my car for a little while. If the journal did mean something to Winona and she left it at home, that pointed more to her being kidnapped than her running away. I looked at the two sketches one last time before starting my car. There was something about the man that made him seem real. He did not seem like a character. I pulled away from the Daughtrys' house and drove home.

3

I WOKE UP EARLY THE NEXT MORNING AND PUT IN A call to Les Myers's home. A woman answered—his mother, I assumed—and when I told her who I was, she said she'd get Les's father on the phone.

"Hello?" he said.

"Hello, Mr. Myers."

"Call me Floyd."

"Okay, Floyd. I'm calling because I need to speak with Les about his—"

"Listen, Les isn't talking to any more schools. He's got his list narrowed down. And besides, you're supposed to go through Coach Freeman before you speak with us."

"No, this isn't about football. I need to speak with Les regarding the matter of Winona Daughtry. She's disappeared."

There was silence on the other end of the line and then a deep sigh from Floyd.

"Look, Les already spoke to the police and told them everything he knows. We have been worried sick over that girl, just like everyone else in town, but this has nothing to do with my son. Please leave us alone. And God help you in your search for that girl." Floyd Myers hung up and the dial tone was static and thick.

I'd expected this sort of response and knew it was going to be difficult to get to Les Myers. The next person I dialed was an old friend named Jerry Calhoun. Jerry was a deputy in the Narcotics Division within the Odessa Police Department. He and I were in the academy together and were both ready to be sworn in before I quit the force the night before the ceremony. Jerry and I remained acquaintances over the next couple of years. He helped me with cases from time to time, and I returned the favor whenever possible. But our past connection was now distant without the common ground of the shield.

Other than Jerry, I hadn't planned on discussing Winona's case with anyone else in the OPD. In my experience, sworn-in officers, especially the rank-and-file cops, found it difficult to talk to a man in my profession.

"Jerry," I said, into the receiver. "How are you? How is Casey and your little baby . . . aw, I'm sorry, what's her name again?"

"Pete!" he said. "It's okay. Her name is Melanie. She and Casey are just fine. Thanks for asking."

"That's fantastic," I said.

"Long time, brother. How's it hanging?"

"I wanted to see if I could take you to lunch today," I said. "How's your twelve o'clock looking?"

There was a pause as Jerry thought. "I could do that for an old friend."

"Max's at twelve?"

"Sounds good."

"See you then," I said.

I hung up and changed into a brown suit, complete with a matching, wide-brimmed, cafe-toned fedora. My plan was to go to the local clinics to find out if Winona had checked in recently to get an abortion. I also planned to talk with Winona's best friend, Courtney Scott, after Courtney got off school. According to Florence, Courtney was Winona's best and most trusted friend and the only one of Winona's friends who had ever set foot in the Daughtrys' house. I left my apartment a little after nine a.m. and hopped into my car.

There were two clinics in Odessa, and they were in the papers often. These two clinics were considered houses of evil to many in Odessa. There had been several protests and even fistfights over the sensitive and complex issue of young girls and their right to choose. When I pulled up to the first address, I was shocked to see that the clinic was permanently closed.

There had been talk in the paper about cutbacks and some clinics having to shutter operations, but there was nothing definitive from what I could recall.

The second address was still live. I parked my car across the street from the squat building and approached. An older woman was standing in front of the entrance. There was a burning in her eyes, which I tried to avoid as I aimed to squeeze past her and into the building. She caught me just in time to put a talon's grip on my shoulder.

"Don't you know that you're committing an abomination against the One, our Lord?" she squawked.

"I'm sorry, Miss," I said in peace.

"Well don't just stand there being sorry! You need to bring yourself to the foot of the Lord. Christ Almighty!" Her grip tightened on my shoulder.

"Please let go of my shoulder, ma'am." Freeing myself from her clutches, I walked inside the clinic. I removed my hat before entering the large waiting room filled with solemn looking faces. The girls, mostly teens from my view, were there in pairs—one with "the issue" and one for support. The clinic employed an appointment system. There were three young women dressed in scrubs behind the front desk that stretched the length of the room. I walked up to the woman who I thought had the nicest face.

"Hello," I said. "I'm looking for any record of a Winona Daughtry having a procedure here. Or of having simply come in here, perhaps."

"And you are?" the smiling woman asked.

I leaned in. "I've been hired by Winona's family. Winona has disappeared, and we recently found out that she was pregnant some time before she disappeared."

"I'm sorry, sir. I can't give you any information about a patient unless you are listed as an emergency contact."

I thought about bringing Florence into it and appealing to the young woman behind the desk on a maternal level. But I remembered that Winona was eighteen—the age of freedom. If Winona had, in fact, checked into the clinic, the woman behind the desk would know her age without a doubt. And from the looks of things at home, Florence would not be listed as Winona's emergency contact.

"How about this?" I said with a theatrical snap. "Can you just tell me whether or not Winona Daughtry was ever a client here? The other clinic was shut down, and I'm assuming that any files they had would've come over here. If you don't have any paper on Winona, that settles it for Odessa. Then at least I'll know to go elsewhere."

"I'm sorry, sir. I can't do it," she said. There was sincerity in her eyes, a sensitivity to my mission of finding *this* girl. I tried to appeal to that sensitivity.

"Look," I said. "I'm not trying to get you into trouble. I just need this one piece of information. I'm trying to find Winona Daughtry for her parents. She may be in danger. She disappeared a week ago, and for all we know, she could be dead. Please. Just give me this one little piece of information and I'll be on my way."

She watched me without speaking, giving me

no choice but to lay it down stronger and more heavy-handedly. "You don't want to get in the way of me finding her, do you?" I asked.

The woman behind the desk looked around to make sure no one else could hear us, and I could see that her eyes were shining. I had hit a nerve with her. I didn't mean to, but wasting time was not an option.

She typed Winona's full name on her keyboard and her eyes perused the results on the screen. She took a couple of minutes before looking back up to me.

"Winona Daughtry was never a patient here or at the other clinic in Odessa—the closed-down one."

"Thank you," I said, with a bow. I walked out of the clinic, and the old woman was still there, busy shaming some other poor soul. I took my cue to get across the street as fast as possible, so that the old lady wouldn't turn her fury back to me. I started up my car and pulled away from the clinic. Winona's decision not to check into Odessa's clinics made sense. If she did have an abortion, she most likely would've had the procedure outside of her hometown. The judgement of others means less in a place where people do not know you personally.

. . . .

I drove east to Midland and found out that one of their two clinics had recently closed as well. When I walked into the operational one, there was an identical setup and clientele. I once again picked the thirty-something young woman behind the front desk, who appeared to be the nicest and went for it.

"I'm sorry, sir. There's no way I could give you this information. I could lose my job," the woman said, with a sweet smile much like her counterpart in Odessa.

I gave this young woman the same spiel as the one in Odessa and received pretty much the same reaction. Her eyes shined at the edges, but instead of punching Winona Daughtry's name on her keyboard, this woman leaned in close, and suddenly we were face to face.

"I have a cigarette break coming up in ten minutes," she said. "Go outside. There's an alley behind the diner three blocks east. I'll meet you there when I take my break."

"Okay," I said. "Thank you." I left and walked outside and past the reincarnation of an old lady condemning blasphemers for simply setting foot in the clinic. I walked to the alley behind the diner and waited. The young woman from behind the desk joined me exactly as she said she would. She lit her cigarette and nodded in the direction of the other end of the alley. We walked.

"I remember that name. I didn't need to look it up." she said. "She first came into the clinic two weeks ago and came in to have the procedure ten days ago."

"Yeah?"

"I was working the day Winona came in for her procedure," she said. "I didn't do her intake that day because I was busy in back with consultations. But I definitely remember her. She was wearing a shirt that said THE VELVETS. Remember The Velvets?"

"Uh-uh."

"They were before my time, but my mom loved The Velvets. She always used to play their records at the house. Anyway, Winona, she's way too young to like or even know about The Velvets. So I asked her about them, you know, to break the ice. And after she explained to me that she just liked the shirt and didn't know the band, we were cool. She was relaxed, and all."

"Did Winona have an abortion that day?"

The young woman nodded and took a long drag off her cigarette. I could hear the tobacco being stretched and roasted as she pulled hard.

"Usually the girls come in with a female friend," she said. "Someone who puts them at ease."

"Who did Winona come in with?"

"A tall, thin man with brown hair down to his shoulders," she said.

I remembered the sketches. "Can you tell me anything else about what happened the day she had her abortion?" I asked, with blood coursing its way to my skull. Even though this case was awful in nature—a missing girl—there is an undeniable rush that comes with the pursuit of information.

The woman from the clinic looked from side to side as if someone else was with us in the empty alley. The sounds of dishes clanging echoed from the opposite end, where the diner stood.

"Winona came in with him and got the procedure."

"Did it seem like they were together?" I asked.

"You mean did they seem like a couple?"

"Yes."

"It seemed like Winona was comfortable with him, if that helps. I don't know what her inner feelings were toward him. She seemed closed off," she said. "But as far as his feeling toward her, I don't know. He was kind of . . . distant."

"What does that mean?"

"A girl just knows. I could tell that she liked him more than he liked her."

"You could tell this just from that day?"

"I see a lot of young girls at the clinic. It's a feeling I got, is all."

"Did Winona seem afraid in any way?"

"Afraid? No, I wouldn't say that. In fact, she was calm before the procedure. A little too calm maybe."

"Like scared?"

"No, not scared. Just calm."

"Sedated?"

The young woman shrugged.

I stepped away from her and paced a couple of steps in each direction. She smoked nervously and checked her watch.

"I don't want to keep you long or put your job in jeopardy," I said. "Can you give me the name of the man she was with?"

She took a final puff and then stamped out the butt underneath her foot. She blew the stream of smoke out in a long string and said, "Johnny Five," she said.

"That's not a real name. It's an alias."

She shrugged again. "Most likely."

"Phone number?"

She shook her head.

"I thought patients are required to leave a phone number for an emergency contact?"

"Before I came out here, I cross-checked the emergency phone number Winona left the day she was in," she said. "Winona wrote down the same phone number under primary contact *and* emergency contact."

"What is the number she wrote?"

She reached into her pocket and produced a scrap of paper. Then she dictated the same cell phone number that Florence had given me for Winona during our initial conversation on the phone. That number was dead.

"Shoot!" I said.

"The person doing Winona's intake that day

should have spotted that there was no true alternate phone number given," she said. "That person screwed up."

"Can I talk to that person? Are they working today?" I asked.

"That person was fired after the mistake was found with Winona's file. The employee had a history of making careless errors."

"Can I have that fired employee's number? Maybe I can get them to talk to me," I said.

"I don't have it," she said. "You'd have to come back inside and wait for me to dig through the old employee files. And I don't think it's a good idea for you to come back inside."

"Did Winona come back in later for a follow-up or to get birth control?"

"No."

"Has the Odessa PD been in to ask questions about Winona being missing?"

She scoffed. "No."

I took a twenty-dollar bill from my wallet and held it out to her.

"What's that for?" she asked.

"For all your help," I said. "I truly appreciate you putting your job on the line for me."

"It's not necessary," she said. "I have to get back. Just make sure you find her."

I pulled the bill away and stuffed it in my pocket.

"Thank you again," I said.

"Good luck."

She started for the other end of the alley.

"Oh!" I shouted. "Miss!"

She turned around.

"I didn't catch your name!"

"Carlene," she said.

"One more thing, Carlene. When you got a look at this Johnny Five that day he came in with Winona," I said. "Was he a young guy?"

"Pretty young," she said, before turning around and exiting the alley.

I drove back into Odessa for my lunch meeting

with Jerry. I went over the strands of the case, and nothing was clear. It all seemed to be stuck together in one nebulous mess. At least I had a name to go along with the sketches now. Johnny Five was the tall, thin, long-haired man from Winona's journal—I was sure of it. He was the man behind the white mask.

4

AX'S HAD BEEN A POPULAR LUNCH COUNTER IN Odessa that had been around for seventy-five years. It was an establishment where a working man of any trade could get a quick bite to eat without the digestive discomfort that comes with fast food. It was also a top lunch spot for cops. I suggested Max's to Jerry because I knew it to be a place where he'd feel at ease.

I took a spot in a corner, two-seat booth. Jerry was five minutes late, which told me that he had something pressing to contend with on his patrol. All the time I'd known Jerry, during and after the academy, punctuality was a quality he possessed. A few of the patrons eyed me, probably recognizing me as a person who was almost a cop, but not quite tough enough to wear the shield. Not quite ready to meet their glares and gazes, I dropped my eyes down to the menu instead.

Jerry walked inside. I could tell it was him from the heavy clicks of his soles as he neared. He was a big, strong man, with cropped blonde hair and clear blue eyes. I stood up and extended my hand to him. Jerry did the same and his demeanor toward me was much different than that of the others in the cafe. He was happy to see me—as always. Jerry knew that I was a worker and that investigation came rather natural for me, regardless of what anyone else thought.

"Pete!" Jerry beamed. "How the hell are you?"

"I'm doing okay. Hope I didn't pull you away from something live."

"Ah! It wasn't that hot. Just a daytime B and E."

"They got Narcotics working a breaking and entering?"

"Department's pressed."

"Any leads yet?" I asked.

Jerry shrugged. "Kids maybe."

I nodded.

"Why don't we sit down and order? I'm starved," he said.

We sat down and he apprised the menu. After we ordered we small-talked a bit more before getting down to it.

"What can I do for you, pal?" he asked before taking a sip of his Arnold Palmer.

"I'm working a case for an old friend back in Fort Stockton."

"Yeah?"

"A married couple, the Daughtrys," I said. "Ever heard of them?"

Jerry shook his head.

"Their daughter, Winona, disappeared nine days ago."

Jerry sighed, as though imagining a scenario in which his daughter Melanie vanished out of the blue.

I took a small flip-notepad out of my jacket pocket and opened it up.

"The parents contacted OPD after two days and filed a report. They said they've been getting the run-around in terms of who in the department is working on Winona's case," I said. "That it's been quote 'a different detective fielding their calls each day,' and beyond that, details have been scarce."

Jerry shifted in his seat as he watched me speak.

"Their frustration led them to hiring me," I said, flipping my notepad shut.

"I'll see who's been assigned to Winona's case," Jerry said without any prompting from me. "And as for the departmental run-around, you know how it is."

I smiled. "Anyway, I'm starting to pull on threads and I've uncovered some things—like her relationship with Les Myers."

"Him I know," Jerry said. "Damn good linebacker.

Smart, instinctive, ain't afraid to stick his nose in there and hit."

"Yeah, well I don't think he has anything to do with Winona's disappearance. His coach—Coach Freeman—wants me to lay off Les. But that doesn't mean anything. He's just protecting his kid. Like I said, I don't think Les has dirt on him."

Jerry watched me as the gears turned inside my head.

"I'd still like to talk with Les," I said.

My old almost-partner still did not speak, and it didn't irk me. The effect was actually the opposite, taking me back to our academy days where we bounced policing ideas off one another.

"I did uncover this other thing regarding Winona and a person named Johnny Five," I said. "Does that name mean anything to you? Maybe you've heard it as 'J-Five' or 'Five-Spot?' '*Cinco*' or something?"

Jerry put his hand underneath his chin and thought. "Johnny Five?"

"A street name maybe?"

"'Five-Spot?'" he asked. "Can't say I've ever heard anything like that, partner."

We were not partners. Ever. But sometimes when I saw Jerry, we'd slip into that routine we had during our academy days. Close to the end of our training, we'd envisioned a future where we would be partners. I'd be the brains and he the brawn.

"It's most definitely an alias," I said. "Think you could find out if this Johnny Five is a drug dealer in town?"

Jerry shook his head up and down as the food arrived. He looked down at his smoked turkey sandwich and then at me. Tacitly, he wanted to know if it was all right that he took a bite of his food before we finished talking. Beneath his tough exterior, Jerry Calhoun was a polite Texas boy who kept hold of his manners.

"Go ahead," I said, with a smile.

Jerry took a bite of his sandwich and then another and another. Just like that, it was gone. He looked across the booth at me.

"Sorry, Pete," he said. "Ain't never heard any name like that in Narcotics."

I reached into my coat pocket. "There's also this." I held out one of the sketches of Johnny Five from Winona's journal—the one with Five sitting in the relaxed pose. I looked at it again and was amazed by how calm the masked figure seemed in the sketch. The subject's tone reminded me of Carlene's appraisal of Winona's friend and his detached demeanor on the day of Winona's procedure. It was unnerving in some way—how relaxed the masked man seemed. Jerry wiped his mouth and fingers and took the sketch for his own examination. His eyes jumped when they focused on the sketch.

"I'm fairly certain that the man in the sketch is Johnny Five," I said. "That mean anything to you?"

"This?" he asked, looking right at the sketch. "Hell no! Spooky looking, ain't it?"

I leaned in; the look in Jerry's eye spoke something else. There was that quick hit of recognition, no matter what he said.

"Jerry," I said. "*This* could be it. This could be the thing that helps me find this girl."

Jerry laughed, "Don't it seem a bit funny though? A masked man? You sure about this, Pete? I ain't never seen a guy like that walking around Odessa." He handed the sketch back to me.

I leaned back in the booth and eyed my old friend.

"This is the kind of thing you see in your dreams," he said. "Nightmares, maybe."

I took a deep breath and looked around the cafe. The other patrons' eyes started to wander over to our booth, and I could sense them closing in on me. They probably wondered what Jerry, a proud cop, was doing with me, a mere private detective. But I knew Jerry better than all of them. He was a good cop but also a showman. He knew how to play the game. If I wanted information, I needed to get after my old friend a little harder and press him about that flash of acknowledgment in his eyes. Something in my gut told me that I had to be tougher, old friend or not.

But Jerry, instinctive as he was, honed in on my indecisiveness and looked me straight in the eye. I heard his harsh nasal breathing—another quirk I recalled from our academy days—and it was shrill and direct. He looked at me dead in the eyes, and I didn't have it in me to return his serve. My eyes moved to the floor and I wasn't able to get what I needed out of him.

"Pete, if that's all, I'm gonna have to be getting back. The paperwork on the B and E is already piling up and threatening to become cold-hearted on me."

I coughed involuntarily. My body suddenly felt hot. The gut-feeling moved swiftly upward, repackaged as cowardice, and introduced itself as a dizziness in my skull. I shook my head to focus my eyes. That helped and I could see Jerry clearly, sitting next to the booth, fitting his hat onto his head.

"You alright, partner?" he asked. "You're sweating like a hog."

"I'm fine," I said, standing up hastily.

"You know, sometimes I wonder how things

would've turned out if you stayed on the force," he said. "Maybe we'd be partners like we planned."

I wiped my forehead with a napkin. It was fully wet after I finished.

"Who knows?" he asked.

"Yeah," I said, now wiping the back of my neck, which was covered in a sheet of sweat. "Who knows?"

Jerry leaned in close. "I'll keep my ear open for this Johnny Five."

"Thanks," I said, with a weak-hearted pat to one of Jerry's broad shoulders.

"I'll be in touch, partner," he said, before walking out of Max's. "Get yourself a cool glass of water or something."

I rushed to the cashier, past the prying eyes, and paid the bill. I burst through the front door of Max's and tried to get around back before the warm, sour slosh lifted out of my stomach, up my throat, and through my mouth. No one else was outside to see the show. There were two more swells until it was all up. My stomach was empty now. I cleaned up with an old handkerchief in my trunk, tossed it in the trash can, and walked around my car to get the dizziness out. I was able to slow everything down and take control.

Jerry knew something about Johnny Five. I couldn't have been surer about anything else in the world. I'd messed up big time by not pressing him harder. I knew that. I just hoped that my weakness wouldn't cost Winona her life. That feeling in my gut from inside Max's—that instinctual, undeniable feeling of connectedness—was now an empty, rotting space inside my center.

5

I HAD TO REDEEM MYSELF IMMEDIATELY FOR MY MIS-
take at Max's. I needed to get to Les Myers.
Though he was all but cleared, I still wanted to
speak with him. At the very least, he and Winona
had a passing relationship. It was a little before
two p.m. on Tuesday when I left lunch with Jerry
Calhoun and regained a composed equilibrium. I
thought of going back to Permian to talk with Les
but decided against it. Crashing Permian's three-
thirty practice was a pointless endeavor on many
fronts. Watching Les go through drills was a waste

of time; plus Coach Freeman made it clear that he wanted me to lay off.

I had my meeting later with Courtney Scott, and with time to spare, I figured another route to get close to Les. I looked up the Myers's Odessa residence using the search engine on my smartphone.

The Myers's home was a two-story colonial type, set far back into the ten thousand block of County Street in old Odessa. The house was made of brick, and the roof looked to be brand new, even though the house was old. I didn't know what Floyd Myers did for a living, but whatever it was, he did well for himself—well enough to have renovated a classic house in old-town Odessa. There was an open gate that surrounded the property and allowed access to the house. The garden was manicured fastidiously, and the plots of lawn on either side of the front door, although small, were clipped to uniformity. I didn't see any cars out front, but that didn't mean the house would be empty. A fancy place like this probably had a garage in back.

I knocked on the front door twice and waited for an answer. After a moment, there were muted steps—soft, the steps of a woman—approaching the door. It opened with a rush of sweet-smelling lotion or shampoo. Lavender. The woman was blonde and built lean, like a greyhound. I could see where Les got his athleticism from.

"Yes?" she called, with lowered eyes.

"Hello."

She quickly appraised me.

"My husband isn't in. Come back later," she said and started to swing the door shut.

"No, it's a misunderstanding," I said. "I'm not here to see your husband."

She fanned the door open again.

"Well?" she said, leaning on one hip now.

"I'm not here to see your husband."

"Yes, yes. You said that already."

"Are you Les Myers's mother?" I asked.

"Yes."

"I need to talk to you about your son."

"What about?"

"There's a situation with Winona Daughtry," I said. "She's been missing for more than a week now. Les was the last person she was with. At least, in public."

She rolled her eyes and her thin face became bitter. "My son would never be caught dead with trash like Winona Daughtry. You have the wrong idea—"

She stopped speaking and blew a stream of air out through her mouth. "I'm sorry," she said, "Les has been cleared. He's already talked to the authorities. We're all hoping that Winona turns up soon." She began to shut the door in my face again.

I kicked my foot into the breach. "Please, Mrs. Myers," I said. "I just need a little bit of your time."

Something I said must've made an impression because she opened the door for a third time.

"Come in then," she said. "Just for a little bit. And call me Claudia. 'Mrs. Myers' makes me sound old."

"Okay."

She walked into her house and left the door open for me. I followed her inside. We entered a sitting room near the back of the house that held a round and rustic wooden table. There was an open window set high up on the wall behind the table.

Claudia turned and faced me. "Would you like a coffee? Or tea?" she asked.

"Coffee would be fine," I said. "Black."

"Fanny!" she called deep into the house.

A minute later, a little old lady materialized. She walked right by me and straight to Claudia.

"Fanny, will you make this gent here a strong, black coffee?" she asked. "I'll have one too if it's not too much trouble. Thank you, dear."

Fanny shambled into the kitchen and started the order. I didn't hear any sounds coming from the kitchen. Fanny worked quietly.

Claudia nodded back to the kitchen.

"The maid," she said. "Makes a hell of a cup of coffee."

I took my hat off and laid it on the table in front of me.

"Sit," she said.

We both sat down, and she continued her appraisal of me from out on her doorstep.

"What are you?" she asked, forgoing the chitchat. "One of those old-time private eyes? Those gents from the dime novels and films?"

"No," I said. "I'm just trying to find Winona."

"You're not dangerous, are you?"

"Dangerous?"

"You seem dangerous."

"I'm not."

She nodded and I responded with a nod of my own. For someone who didn't want to give me a lot of time, she sure took her sweet time.

"You wanted to talk about my son?" she asked, after our circular exchange.

"Yes, about his relationship with Winona."

"Let me ask you something, Mr . . . " she said. "I'm sorry, I didn't catch your name at the door."

"I never gave it," I said.

"Mr. . . . ?"

"Pete. Pete Hamilton."

"Pete," she said. "Do you think this is the right place to come for information about Winona Daughtry?"

"I don't follow," I said.

"I mean, why aren't you at the Daughtry residence right now?"

Fanny approached holding a tray with two cups of coffee set on it. She served Claudia first. Fanny then placed my cup in front of me and still failed to acknowledge me, even though I greeted her kindly with my eyes. Fanny left us again.

"You should give me a bit more credit than that," I said. "I've been to see the Daughtrys, and the job has brought me here."

"Job?" she asked. "And what is it exactly that you do?"

"Do? I told you earlier. I find people."

She nodded theatrically as she blew on her

steaming coffee. She took a warning sip and then a bigger one. She left a smudge of cherry-red lipstick on the rim of her cup.

"I don't want to waste your time," I said. "Do you know anything about your son seeing Winona Daughtry?"

She waved at the air lazily.

"Les is a teenage boy. And a star athlete. I don't know exactly how many girls he's been seeing. I can't even tell you for certain that he's seen any girls."

"How is that possible?"

"Because I'm not the most effective mother, Pete. Certainly no candidate for 'Mother of the Year,'" she said. "Don't get me wrong. I'm here for Les. I take care of him. I go to all of his football games." She paused. "I guess I don't really *know* my son all that well."

Her words first punched me in the face and then went to work on my body. She had knocked the wind out of me. The barrage diverted my mind back to Florence Daughtry. The similarities between her and Claudia, though not exactly synced up, held enough in common to denote a pattern that was only gathering steam. Two different worlds, two different mothers, but a strikingly similar sentiment about their children. It was true that neither mother really knew her offspring.

"If you would like specifics on Les, it's better to ask Floyd. Floyd's his father," she said.

"Your husband won't talk to me."

"Probably not," she said, before another sip. "Drink your coffee. Fanny's the best."

"Forget about the coffee," I said. "I have to talk with Les."

"Talk to Floyd," she said.

I stood up and put on my hat, turning to leave. Then I remembered the sketches and reached into my pocket to pull them out.

"Do these mean anything to you?" I asked, handing the folded sheets over to her.

Claudia Myers took the pages and unfolded

them. Her left pointer finger traced the edge of one of the sketches as the right hand held the page close to her face. Unlike Jerry Calhoun, there was no recognition in her eyes at the bizarre sight of the masked man with shoulder-length hair. There was something funny about it to her, however. She giggled like a teenager.

"What's funny?" I huffed, with my hands dug deep into my pockets.

"Oh nothing," she said. "I just remember when I was girl, the kinds of ridiculous things I doodled in my journal."

I leaned over and snatched the sketches out of her hand, and her eyes cut into me.

"This *girl*," I said, "is missing."

"Most likely, she hasn't been kidnapped, Pete," Claudia said. "She's run off and when she's done, when this current fixation has run its course in her mind, she'll be back."

I turned and let myself out of the Myers's house.

I drove to my meeting with Winona's best friend, Courtney.

6

PERMIAN LET OUT AT THREE P.M., SO I SET MY
meeting with Courtney at three forty-five. I
understood that it wasn't easy for a teenager, especially a female one, to talk to me, so I wanted to give
Courtney a bit of time to relax and gather herself
before our meeting. Courtney's parents were hesitant
to allow her to meet with me at first, but she was able
to convince them that she had to do it for Winona.
That's what Courtney's mother told me over the
phone anyway.

The meeting was to take place at my office. I
arrived there around three fifteen. My encounter with

Claudia only reinforced the fact that it was going to be tough to locate Winona. The folks in town, especially those close to Permian football, weren't going to go out of their way to help me. I hadn't learned anything new after setting foot in the Myers's house. That had been a waste of time. I would have to continue devising new ways to get to Les Myers. I had a hunch that he was the key to figuring all this out.

At three forty-five sharp there was a knock on my office door. I let Courtney and her mother inside and motioned for them to sit. I walked around my desk and sat down across from them. Courtney had the unmistakable look of one of the popular girls at school. That threw me because I didn't get the impression from the Daughtrys that Winona was running with Permian's in-crowd. Florence described Winona as being right in the middle when it came to social standing, a chameleon of sorts—a girl who could fit in temporarily with different cliques, but ultimately without the staying power of full acceptance by a single tribe.

Courtney's appearance said otherwise: long, flowing black hair, clear skin, green eyes. It would be no surprise that she dated a football player.

"Thank you for coming here to talk to me," I said to both of them.

"No problem," Courtney said. "Can I ask a question?"

"Sure," I said.

"Does my mom have to be in here while we talk?"

"She doesn't have to be," I said. "But because you're a minor, she has to agree to leave the room *and* sign any statement that you give."

Courtney's mother sat stone-faced during her daughter's and my dialogue.

"But I'm not a minor," Courtney said, happily. "I turned eighteen last Saturday."

I looked at Courtney's mother and saw her demeanor was set. Clearing my throat I said, "Well, Courtney, even though you are eighteen, I still think it's right to get your mother's permission for you to talk to me alone."

"Okay, Mom," Courtney said, turning to her mother. "Can you leave the room, please? Let me talk to him so he can find 'Nona."

Finally, a perceptible reaction from Mrs. Scott. She looked at me with something just short of fear—trepidation maybe. Even though I was trying to find a missing teenage girl, I understood Mrs. Scott's acquittal of me. After meeting with the Daughtrys and Claudia Myers, Mrs. Scott's active concern regarding her daughter's life was a welcome sight.

I sat patiently and waited for mother and daughter to hash it out.

Mrs. Scott looked back at Courtney and stood up. "Fine," she said and turned to me. "Please don't take longer than twenty minutes."

I nodded. "Yes, ma'am."

Mrs. Scott left the room, and the change of tone inside was sudden. Courtney and I acknowledged our shared relaxation with an exchange of glances.

She stood up and took out a pack of cigarettes from the front left pocket of her jeans.

"You mind?" she asked.

"No."

I reached into the top drawer of my desk and took out an ashtray. I placed it in front of her as she lit the cigarette.

"I'm glad my Mom left the room," Courtney said before taking her first drag.

"Don't talk like that, Courtney," I said. "This is a bad situation, and she's just concerned for you."

"This stuff with 'Nona is messed up," she said.

I couldn't help but think of the sketches of Johnny Five and the sadness in the Daughtry house. "What's messed up?" I asked. "The fact that she's missing or the circumstances of Winona's life?"

"You tell me?" she replied, with a wave of her cigarette.

I saw a sign of maturity in Courtney Scott's eyes and decided to double down on it. I was running out of time as it was, beating around the bush and getting nowhere. With these kinds of cases—disappearances or kidnappings—time is the great enemy. And I was already far behind—maybe too far behind.

"Well, what do you mean?" I persisted. "Is it that Winona carried on a secret relationship with one of Permian's best football players? I can't get anyone in Odessa to talk to me about Winona's relationship with Les Myers. *Or* is it that Winona recently went to a clinic in Midland to get an abortion?"

Courtney had finished her cigarette by the time I finished speaking. To her credit, she didn't sweat. The whole thing seemed easy for her.

"You look very young to be doing this kind of work," she said. "How old are you?"

"I don't have time to mess around, Courtney!" I said, standing up from my desk. I approached her. "Now if you want me to find your friend, you need to give me some information! If you don't, please get out of my office and stop wasting my time, because every second I'm not out there looking makes it harder for me to find Winona."

At this point, I was almost looming over Courtney. Her breath quickened, and I remembered that this was a young person that I was talking to. Her cool act was just that, an act. I put my head in my hands and walked away from the desk. I took a deep breath and collected my thoughts.

"I'm sorry, Courtney," I said. "I'm sorry. Today was a rough one for me. I have no right to talk to you like that. You're here to help me find your friend."

She was quiet. I'd spooked her good but I was confident I'd get her back.

"She is your friend, right?" I asked.

She nodded.

There was a heavy silence between us now. I walked over to the mini-fridge in the corner of the office and took out two bottled waters. I made my way back over to the desk and held one of the bottles out to her.

"Here," I said.

She took the bottle from me.

"Thank you," she said.

I opened my bottle and took a long, thoughtful drink, nearly finishing it. Even though I hadn't really eaten that day, I wasn't hungry. This case was nourishing me in a way. I hadn't taken the time to eat a decent meal because of it. The more I learned—or didn't learn—about Winona Daughtry, the further I drifted away.

"Winona started hanging around this guy called the Moon," Courtney said out of nowhere. "Some time last year, when we were juniors. I'm not positive when."

The Moon. Johnny Five. The sketches. "Tell me about him," I said.

"Everybody knows about the Moon in Odessa," she said. "At least everyone at Permian and Odessa High."

"Does he sell drugs?" I asked.

"Yes."

"What kind of drugs does he sell?"

"All kinds."

"Be specific, Courtney."

"Weed, pills, and I think heroin too."

"Is Winona strung out on heroin, Courtney?" I asked. "I know it's hard to talk about this, but I need to know."

Her eyes watered and tears streamed out of them like a faucet. The flow of tears was rather thick and constant. I reached into the second drawer of my desk and pulled out a box of tissues. I handed her a few and gave her time to wipe her eyes and collect herself. I didn't like making her cry, but I couldn't let up. I couldn't make the same mistake I had made earlier in the day.

"Is she strung out?" I repeated. "Is Winona hooked on heroin, Courtney?"

She blew her nose into the wad of tissues and then searched for a trash can. I pointed to the corner of the room. She spotted the receptacle, stood up, and tossed the tissues into it. She walked back and sat down.

"That's not it," she said, blowing air out of her mouth. "That's not it."

"What else? What else is there, Courtney?"

There was a knock at my door. It was Mrs. Scott. I looked down at Courtney and put a finger up to my lip.

"Shh," I whispered.

I walked over to the door and opened it. Mrs. Scott's attitude was more or less the same as when she was in the office earlier.

"Twenty minutes is up, Mr. Hamilton."

"Mrs. Scott, Courtney is right in the middle of telling me something that I believe will lead me to Winona. I just need a little more time."

She looked past me and into the office. Courtney had her back to us.

"Court!" Mrs. Scott called into the office. "Are you okay? Do you want to stop talking to him?"

"I'm fine, Mom," she said, with all the tear-induced residue miraculously cleared out of her sinuses and throat. "He's gonna find Winona."

"Okay. Walk her down when you-all are finished," Mrs. Scott said. "I'm parked across the street."

"I will," I said. "Thank you, Mrs. Scott."

Mrs. Scott left again and I closed the door. Her mother's appearance seemed to calm Courtney. I was calm now too. We had a trust in each other because we both wanted the same thing: Winona home safe.

I sat down in the chair next to Courtney instead of sitting across from her or standing over her. I had to take the feeling of interrogation out of our conversation.

"Winona is wild," Courtney said, unprompted, "but things didn't get crazy until the Moon came into the picture."

"You have to be more specific, Courtney," I said.

I pulled out the sketches and fanned them open for Courtney to see.

"Is this the Moon, Courtney?" I said. "Is this him?"

She averted her eyes from the sheets at first. I moved them closer to her face, and she looked at them. Her eyes didn't change. She nodded.

"What's with his face?" I said. "Is it a mask?"

"Yes. The sketches are probably from the night Winona met the Moon at last year's Permian Halloween party. She's an awesome artist. She draws a lot but doesn't really talk about it. I guess that's probably not helpful."

I jotted this down on a small notepad that sat on my desk.

"It is. Every detail is helpful. What did you mean when you said things got 'crazy'?" I asked.

She paused and there was a weight to it. She knew that once these next words exited her lips, she'd never get them back.

"It's okay," I said. "You can trust me."

"She just . . . she just started sleeping with a lot of guys around the same time she met the Moon."

"What's a lot?"

"*A lot*," she said. "I mean, I'm no prude. I've had sex. But not like Winona has."

"Be specific."

"I don't know. Ten, fifteen, maybe twenty guys."

I jotted a note.

"What do you mean by 'guys'? You mean men?" I asked.

"People from Permian, players mostly. Also some men from Odessa and Midland."

Midland. The clinic. Johnny Five and the Moon were the same person.

"What can you tell me about her and Les?" I asked. "Was Les the father?"

"I don't know about that, honestly," she said. "Our friendship wasn't great this past year. She wasn't truthful with me. And like I said, there were a lot of candidates. It could have been anyone's."

"How do you know about all these people she slept with if your friendship with Winona wasn't on good terms this past year?"

"Because I was at the parties," she said. "The parties are where it all goes down."

"And the Moon goes to these parties?"

"Yes," she said.

"Was Les the last person that Winona was with before she disappeared?"

"You mean were they together? Like a couple?"

"I mean sex." I said.

"No. That was the reason that Les freaked out over Winona. He found out she was seeing other guys."

"It wasn't that she was pregnant with his child?"

"I can't say that for sure," she said with a deep breath. "I was with Winona the night before she left, and I could just tell that something was about to happen with her. I could *feel* it. There was this poisonous feeling between us. We never talked about it, but it was there. We were in the bathroom together at the Permian party after the Abilene game, two Friday nights ago. That's the last time I saw her."

She began to cry again, this time putting her face into her hands. I patted her back gently.

"Okay," I said. "It's okay. I have to talk to Les. Do you think you can get me into this Friday's Permian party?"

I reached over and grabbed a couple more tissues. She lifted her head and took them, blowing her nose again. She thought for a moment as she wiped her face, but after a few more sobs, her eyes steeled, and she turned the tears off like a faucet. There was a strength inside her that was rising—a strength to do the right thing, even though it was the difficult thing.

"Yes. I can get you in," she said.

"Permian plays Friday, right?"

"Against Midland," she said.

"Do you know where the party will be?"

"Not yet," she said. "The location isn't set until right before the game on Fridays."

"What? Why?"

She shrugged. "The cops."

"What does that mean?"

"It means that the cops are always trying to break up our parties. The longer the location of the party stays a secret, the longer it takes the cops to arrive. You know, it's hard to hit a moving target, type of thing."

I nodded and wrote this down on the notepad.

"Okay," I said, taking one of my business cards

out of its holder on my desk. I handed my notepad over to her. "Write your cell phone number on here and take one of my cards."

She took a pen from the desk, wrote her number down on the notepad, and handed it back to me.

"When you find out about the party's location on Friday, you text me," I said.

She nodded. I handed her the business card to keep for herself.

"My cell number is on there."

"Will you be at the game on Friday?" she asked.

"I'm not sure yet," I said. That was a lie. Even though she was helping me, Courtney was still a high school girl. I didn't know if she'd go over to some friend's house after leaving my office and spill the whole thing. I would go to the game and follow Permian's players to the party afterward as a fail-safe. But Courtney needed to feel included as well.

"I'll rely on you for the party's location," I said.

A look of pride came into her eyes.

"Thank you," I said. "I won't be able to find Winona without you."

"I have to go," she said.

I followed her to the door. "One last question."

She turned with a sigh.

"These guys that Winona was with. Were they mostly football players?"

"Yes," she said. "The Moon likes football and loves hanging out with football players."

Before I was able to reply, Courtney walked out of my office without me. I followed her down the hallway and caught up. It didn't really matter if she walked downstairs alone, but I didn't want to break my promise to Mrs. Scott.

On the way down to the lobby and then to Mrs. Scott's car, Courtney and I didn't say another word. I didn't know exactly where this was going, but I had a feeling that it was going somewhere bad. Something was happening with young girls in Odessa. Courtney's mother was right to be protective of her child.

I opened and closed the car door for Courtney,

and they pulled away from the curb. I watched them until their car made a right turn a few blocks up. My vision tilted upward; the sky was slate gray with a brewing, ornery cloud right above me. It threatened an unforeseen rain.

The Moon was dangerous. He was drawing in young girls and taking advantage of them, using them to a nub and then most likely discarding them. I had to find out how he did it. And I had to stop him.

7

I CALLED THE DAUGHTRYS EARLY THE NEXT MORNING and updated them as best I could with what I had so far: hypothetical, tangential theories, and all. They didn't think much of my news, but Florence was thankful that I had actually called. I reiterated my intention to find Winona, and Florence cried again before hanging up. I thought about calling Floyd Myers and giving him another run but decided not to. I would get to Les at the Permian party.

My plan was to set up a drug buy from the Moon, or—at the very least—one of his people. I gave Jerry Calhoun a call to fill him in on my new information about the Moon. It was all news to him. Once again unprompted, Jerry promised me that he wouldn't spread the revelatory news of the Moon across the department just yet. I agreed with that course because I needed a little time to find Winona. News of a predatory drug dealer would send the OPD on a hunt for blood and headlines, leaving Winona Daughtry an unfortunate afterthought. Jerry ended the phone call by calling me "partner" again.

I had a couple of guys on the street that I went to when I needed information on dope peddlers, pimps, and the like. One of my most reliable guys, Leon Mendocino, had helped me find a runaway girl all the way over in San Antonio two years back. Leon was trustworthy, even though he was a recovering addict-turned-snitch. But he'd been MIA for the last month or so.

With Leon out of touch, I planned to use a fellow by the name of Dennis for information on the Moon. Dennis never told me his last name, and that was fine by me. Reliance on Dennis was a tricky proposition;

his information had been hit or miss over the two years that we worked together.

Finding Dennis was also no easy task. It usually took me a few days of scouring Odessa's bars, lounges, and pool halls before he turned up. But I didn't have a few days in this case. I had to be right on the first try.

I got dressed in a dark blazer over an even darker button-down shirt—my outfit matching my mood, my mood matching the tenor of the case. I drove over to the Note, an old dive in east Odessa. The Note was famous for opening at nine in the morning. Only the most dedicated patrons frequented the Note—those with true dedication to the craft of day drinking. I knew Dennis to be a loyal client, so I checked there first. I walked in and spoke to the bartender, Lorene. She hadn't seen Dennis that morning yet, but had seen him the day before. I gave Lorene five dollars, took a seat in a back booth, and hoped to get lucky. After an hour and fifteen minutes, Dennis strolled in with that unmistakable swagger a day drinker holds before that first, reckoning sip.

Lorene came over, talked into his ear, and pointed to me in the back booth. Dennis turned around and spotted me. I could see him curse under his breath. He ordered a drink and walked over to my booth with his head down. He looked like a scolded child. I slid to the middle of the circular booth and gave him room to slide in on either side.

"What it is, Pete?" he asked, before slurping the foam off his morning beer.

"Hello Dennis."

"I'm a little busy today, Pete," he said. "You got a stog, by the way?"

I lifted a pack of cigarettes out of the breast pocket of my blazer. I always kept them on hand when planning to talk to informants.

I handed the pack over to Dennis.

"Keep it," I said.

He slid a cigarette out of the pack, popped it into

his mouth and used the tabletop candle to light it. He blew a long stream of smoke over my head.

"How have you been?" I asked.

"Aw, I can't complain," he said. "Haven't seen you around for a while. I figured maybe you drifted into some other line of work."

"No," I said. There was a constant nervousness to Dennis that was palpable. I knew him to be a fidgety man, but he was even more so on this day.

"Say, have you seen Leon around town lately?" I asked, trying to get a line into my more reliable man.

"Leon? Nah," he said. "Might've skipped."

"Left Odessa for good?"

"Folks is always getting lost. Losing themselves and finding themselves again," he said, thoughtfully.

I nodded, and the smoke drifting up from his cigarette was suddenly the only thing between us. Each time Dennis and I crossed paths like this it was the same. We had to play this game. He wasn't going to voluntarily submit himself for snitch work.

"I need something, Dennis," I said finally.

"I gotta know what it is first, and I'll see what I can do, Pete," he said, like always.

"You ever heard the name Johnny Five around Odessa? That or the Moon?"

He took a philosophical pull on his cigarette, giving off a look of deep contemplation.

"Johnny Five?" he asked.

"Yeah."

He shook his head quickly.

I wasn't buying it. The two names registered in his mind. I didn't have the time or patience to deal with his routine. "You know, Dennis," I said, "if you know anything, anything at all about Johnny Five or the Moon, you'd better tell me. My friend on the force is the one assigned to that B and E from yesterday. And his ass is on the line. His sergeant is leaning on him. Hard."

I watched as Dennis's eyes came alive. With surgical precision, my eyes feigned wistfulness. "I seem to remember that you have a skill set for breaking into houses," I said. "You had the whole operation covered if I recall correctly. You'd scope the house for a few days, make sure you pinned down their schedules, and then you'd crack a window and pick the house clean."

Dennis ground out his cigarette in the ashtray and tried to get up from the booth. Grabbing him by the wrist, I squeezed until I felt the tendons crunch. I tossed him onto the table, sending the glasses and candle to scatter along the floor. I leaned in close to his face. My heart rate spiked.

"Does all that sound familiar to you, Dennis? Huh?" I snarled. The rest of the bar was radio silent and tuned into what was happening at the back booth. But I didn't care. I was through wasting time.

"Do I have the right person, Dennis?"

"You're crazy!" he said. "Get offa me!"

"This is no game," I said, both hands around his collar now, shaking him like a tree, as if the answer I was looking for would simply fall out of him if I shook hard enough. "There's a girl missing because of this guy Johnny Five. If you don't tell me what you know about him, I swear I'll serve you up to the OPD myself."

"Okay!" he screamed. "But I don't know no Johnny Five, Pete!"

I shook him one more time.

"Just let go of me so I can talk."

I let go of his collar and slumped down into the booth. The bar was quiet—museum-like—as if no one inside dared to move for fear of my wrath. My hands shook, and it took a second for me to get them under control. Dennis writhed on the table like a hooked fish, begging to be clubbed.

"I do know the Moon," he whispered.

I stared at him as I tried to gather my breathing. Once it slowed to something close to normal, I walked over to the bar, asked Lorene for a glass of water, guzzled the entire glass, and returned to the booth. By the time I came back, Dennis was sitting in the booth with another lit cigarette. I sat next to him. Our eyes were straight ahead. Neither of us blinked.

"I'll help you," he said, unprompted. "But I'm warning you now. You're barking up an evil tree with this. An evil goddamned tree."

8

DENNIS AND I LEFT THE NOTE SHORTLY AFTER THE altercation. We got into my car, and he gave me directions to a house on the west side of Odessa. This part of town was rough, with most of the houses in dilapidated condition.

"Just keep straight up here and make a left when I say to," Dennis said, without moving his eyes off the windshield.

This part of Odessa was known as a narcotics hotbed. I remembered this from the directives during my time in the academy. There was also the occasional violent crime that happened here, as well as all of the other things that came with the drug trade: poverty, prostitution, and general decay.

"Hook a left," he said.

I turned the car, and after passing two more blocks with broken-down homes, Dennis fixed his eyes onto a two-level, brown house outside the passenger window. He raised his left hand and tapped my right arm.

"Stop here," he said.

I parked the car in front of the brown house. When Dennis unbuckled his seatbelt, I didn't. He looked over at me.

"Well?" he asked. "What you waitin' on?"

"I need to know what we're getting into here," I said. "Is there danger inside this house?"

Dennis flashed a charming smile—one that probably did wonders for him out on the streets. "Man, you wanted to know what I knew about the Moon, but when I give you what you want, you all flip-floppin'," he said.

"This is where the Moon lives?" I asked.

He chuckled and found it necessary to continue laughing for a minute or so. "Nah, you wanted to know what I knew about the Moon," he said. "The people in that house are my only connections to the Moon."

Dennis stabbed a pointer finger toward the brown house. "I ain't never heard about no Moon until my dude in there put me onto his stuff."

"You cop heroin from the Moon?" I asked.

Dennis's eyes widened. "Well you could say that. The Moon supplies my man in there."

I looked past Dennis and through the passenger window at the brown house.

"Just tell me what you want, boss, 'cause you got me confused."

"Are they armed? The people inside?"

"Yeah they're armed. But my man, Ox, he ain't no banger. He carries a piece more for . . . what you call it?" Dennis thought before snapping his fingers on revelation. "The shock effect."

I had my .38 Special nestled in the shoulder

holster underneath my blazer. It was loaded, with a bullet in the breech. My dark blazer had been tailored to hide the bulge. It must have been done right because Dennis made no reference to it.

"We goin' in or what, Pete?" Dennis demanded.

"Yeah."

We got out of the car and slammed our doors shut in unison. Dennis led the way up the stone walk toward the house. There was a metal security guard over the front door, its grille rusted and flecked with old dirt. Dennis pounded on the guard three times. I looked up furtively and saw a small hole that was drilled into the frame above the metal guard. That would be a camera. The Moon and his associates were careful men.

Dennis knocked two more times before a man dressed in all black opened the front door of the house and looked out at us. He was a big man, and looked athletic. His head was shaved, and his face was young—young and familiar. I knew him from somewhere but couldn't be sure of his identity because of the metal between us.

The man sighed after his appraisal of Dennis and me.

"Whatchu want, Dennis?" he asked.

His voice carried the cautious importance of just leaving pubescence in the rear view. He was a young man, maybe fresh out of high school.

"I need to get with Ox," Dennis said.

"Who's your man?" the bald young man asked, nodding at me.

"This is a friend of mine—an associate," Dennis said, before coughing. "He's got a line to some weight."

I played it cool even though Dennis and I hadn't discussed a specific way to get us inside. One thing that Dennis and I did share was a chemistry for improvisation. His instincts were sound. These people were in charge of a drug operation. Why else would they talk to me if it wasn't about drugs?

The bald young man gave me another appraising

look and then unlocked the metal guard. When I got a better look at his face, I recognized who he was—Tyrone Mack, a star linebacker at Permian High two years prior. From what I could remember from the papers, Mack had his choice of three or four scholarships in Texas alone. That was before he tore up his knee in the final game of his senior season at Permian. Seeing him in front of me led me to believe that the scholarship offers were rescinded, and without college and the prospect of the NFL, Mack had to find a new way to survive.

"I gotta frisk him though," Mack said.

Mack reached into the breast pocket of my blazer and extracted my cell phone.

"You don't mind, right?" he asked.

When he found the revolver in my shoulder holster, he pulled it out and examined it. He smiled and asked, "What the hell did you think you was gonna do with *this*?"

I shrugged. "You know how it is," I said.

"Yeah. I do," Mack said. "I'm gonna have to hold

onto these until your business with Ox is finished. You understand that, right?"

"Yes," I replied.

Mack opened the door and stood aside for Dennis and me to enter. He looked out to the street before closing and locking the metal guard door, and then threw the deadbolt on the front door.

The inside of the house was more or less what I'd envisioned when I first saw its exterior. The pungent musk of marijuana smoke hung in the air. There were two large paper bags filled with empty beer bottles and liquor handles by the front door. There was what looked like a living room to the left of the front door, with a large, L-shaped, black leather couch and a flat-screen TV hanging on the far wall. There was an older black man sitting on the couch with a black female next to him. The female looked young—either still in, or fresh out of high school—and she wore a bikini top and cut-off jeans. The two of them stared at Dennis and me as we stood in the foyer.

"Come on," Mack said.

We followed Mack through a hallway that led into the kitchen. The floors were clean but the rest of the room was filthy. That threw me. If the kitchen was the place where they prepared the drugs, the entire room should've been clean. But there were pizza boxes and old Chinese carry-out containers everywhere. More empty beer bottles and candy wrappers dotted the counters too. Mack walked through the kitchen, and we continued on his heels.

When we reached a steel-enforced door that screamed *drug depot*—either the counting room or inventory stash—Mack pulled a heavy-duty key out of his front pocket and stuck it into the lock. It turned with a dramatic *clunk*, and even though Mack was a physical specimen, he grunted as he pushed the door open. He stepped aside again to let Dennis and me pass through, and when we entered, the light inside was low, bordering on nonexistent. There were empty desks on either side of the steel door. Both desks had money-counting machines that you'd see in banks along with accountant calculators. This was where they counted the money, and this man, Ox, was someone high up in the Moon's organization. If the Moon trusted him with the money, Ox may have even been second in command.

In the far corner of the back room was a set of four chairs with high backs. The chairs were situated around a high-legged, glass coffee table, and there was a globe light overhead, emitting a pale, almost smoldering glow. This was the only source of light in the room. As Dennis, Mack, and I moved closer to the table, I saw a man and woman sitting in two of the chairs. The woman was white and young. She had dirty blonde hair. I locked in quickly to see if it was Winona Daughtry. It was not.

Once again, clinging to the theme of the house, I saw she was of high school age, not a woman at all. The man sitting next to her was black and wore sunglasses. His hair was dreadlocked, and his gold-capped front teeth glinted in the overhead globe.

Mack led us to the table, where we stood before Ox. There was a rectangular shaving mirror dusted with a brown residue and a rolled-up dollar bill on the table.

With a closer look, I realized that the young female was, in fact, a girl. Her cheeks reddened with the attention given to her, and her braces were a dead giveaway. Ox kept his attention on the girl even though he saw us enter and approach. I masked my personal feelings as best as I could while Ox and the girl continued their dalliance, and Ox didn't notice a thing. He finally acknowledged us with a sideways glance.

"Baby, why don't you give the men here a chance to talk for a split second?" Ox said.

The girl giggled, stood up, and yawned. She passed Dennis and me and quickly became lost in the darkness of the room. Mack followed her. He strained to open and close the steel door.

"Dennis," Ox asked. "You need a little somethin'?"

Dennis shifted tentatively. "Nah, Ox. I was

hoping to get with you for a minute. I know you're busy."

Ox fed off Dennis's compliments. He grinned like a king.

"This is my man, Tolbert," Dennis said, clapping me on the back.

I don't know where Dennis got the name from but it worked. Ox didn't bat an eye. Mack joined from behind.

"Tolbert, huh?" Ox said. "Well why don't y'all take a seat."

Mack took the seat right next to Ox—the one the girl had been sitting in. Dennis and I sat across from them.

Ox chuckled to himself and then playfully backhanded Mack's bulging right bicep.

Mack glared across the table at Dennis and me. It was clear that Mack was more than muscle. He didn't feed into Ox's more laid-back and silly attitude because he didn't have to. In fact, Mack's demeanor read that he was higher up in the organization than his physique implied.

"What's the play here, Dennis?" Mack asked, with steel in his eyes. "Don't be wastin' our time."

"I'm gonna let Tolbert here take over, fellas," Dennis said, shamefaced. "I'm just the messenger."

"Dennis has been telling me for a couple years now about his friends in Odessa that are doing things," I said.

"Where you from, Tolbert?" Ox asked.

"Midland."

"You known Dennis for years?" Mack inquired.

"Me and Dennis go way back—"

"Dennis is older than you," Mack jumped in. "How you two even know each other?"

I knew this response could either blow my cover or extend the game further. I thought about it hard—but quickly. In the academy, they taught that when working undercover, you *always* have to think hard and quick. And do not—ever—let them *see* that you are thinking.

"I used to sell him nickel bags when he'd come out Midland way," I said.

"When y'all wouldn't give a nigga no more stuff on credit," Dennis chimed in with a warm smile, helping my cause.

Ox and Mack were satisfied, and suggested with their silence that I continue with my proposition.

"I made it through my time as a hustler, and I'm still here," I said.

This seemed to resonate more with Ox than it did with Mack, telling me that Ox was a career drug dealer and that Mack was not.

I quickly recalled the list of drugs that Courtney Scott had rattled off during my meeting with her the day before. I remembered that she hadn't mentioned cocaine as a drug that the Moon specialized in.

"I got a connect in El Paso that's supplying me with a half-kilo of raw in a week or so," I said.

"Ho, ho, ho," Mack said. "Dennis, you tell this dude that we into selling coke?"

I jumped in at the opportunity. "That's why I

wanted to talk you gents. I know you got dope on lock. There's big money to be made in powder. Coke's making a comeback, *right now*. And you can cut it five, six times, and it'll still have the fiends coming back for more."

I could feel Dennis's eyes on me as I spoke. He had never heard me talk like they do on the streets. I carried it well though. Ox and Mack were engaged.

"There's a lot of questionable powder from Mexico, Tolbert," Ox said. "We don't want none of that."

"The coke I'm talking about is pure, Ox," I said. "My connect works with the Colombians."

Ox's eyes lit up. There are certain words that legitimize you in the minds of drug dealers, and "Colombians" is one of them. Mack, on the other hand, was not impressed. It was difficult for me to figure out just where he fit into all of this.

"I need your distribution for my supply," I said.

"We'd have to try a sample," Mack said. "*Test* if the stuff is raw."

Ox nodded.

"That's not a problem," I said. "I don't have a taste on me because I never carry it when I drive."

This impressed Ox as well.

"I can make that happen, though, if we decide to work together," I said.

Mack stood up. "Well you need to slow your roll with all that. We don't just let white boys stroll in here and run things."

The Moon flashed into my mind just then—a white boy "running things."

"You hear me, white boy?" Mack asked.

Mack's frame was imposing, especially with the halo of light over him. It was no accident that he stood over me, looking down with clenched fists, tense limbs, and discerning eyes. I looked up to him and nodded.

"I gotta talk to my man before we go anywhere else with this," Mack said. "I'll get word back to Dennis if we even get to that point."

Mack left the table and walked out of the small

radius of light. "Besides," Mack said, as he walked away. "You got a test to pass from Ox before you even think of getting to my man."

"And who is your man, Mack?" I asked to his back.

The sound of Mack opening and closing the steel door shook the room.

"Don't mind Mack," Ox said, with a sniff. "He misses scaring the piss out of people on the football field. Now he scares people around here when he gets the chance."

"What's the test?" I asked.

"Yeah, the test," Ox said. "It's the test that every-one has to pass. Dennis passed with flying colors a couple years back."

I looked over at Dennis, and he nodded with something close to sadness in his eyes. Regret maybe. This was the first time I ever associated those emotions with Dennis.

"What is it?" I asked again.

"Well I don't really know how y'all like to get

down in Midland," Ox said, with a blinding glimmer off his gold-caps. "But you're about to find out how we do it here in Odessa."

9

Ox, Dennis, and I were in the living room sitting on the L-shaped couch. Mack was out of sight. I wasn't sure if he'd left the house or was just in another room. I heard the faint sounds of footsteps on the carpet overhead, though.

"What are we doing?" I asked after a period of lazy silence.

"Hey, Tolbert," Ox said, tilting his sunglasses down. "Chill with the questions. Get me thinkin' you a cop."

I didn't reply.

"Besides. We're gonna do what we always do

here," Ox said. "Gonna order some food. Gonna get high."

"And?" I said, with a bit more edge than I aimed to exude.

"And, you're gonna participate," Ox said. "If you wanna do business with us, you gotta get high. And you got to get with one of our girls."

I stared at Ox, and he stared back at me with a foolish and rehearsed grin. He shrugged his shoulders.

"Ain't no other way around it," he said. "Call it 'insurance' for us."

I nodded. "Yeah, that's fine. I wasn't planning on workin' anymore today."

"Good, good," Ox said. "Now I know what Dennis wants. But what's your poison, Tolbert?"

I thought hard and quick again. I had smoked marijuana back in high school a few times, and it never became a habit. Other than beer, which I enjoyed casually, I had no go-to mind-altering substance.

"Why don't you roll up some of that weed I smell?" I asked.

"That's not gonna do the trick," Ox said. "You gotta show us a little more than that. I need to know for sure that you ain't no cop."

Ox took a bundle of small ziplock bags out of the front left pocket of his jeans. He tossed the bundle onto the coffee table in front of the couch. It was heroin—I could tell from its pale, brown color. Dennis's eyes lit up and it was all he could do not to pounce on it. Ox watched me and not Dennis. I was the variable here. He knew Dennis. I looked Ox right in the eye and smiled—not because I knew of some way to keep myself clean in all this, but because I thought it was the only way to keep the game going. I thought about Winona before opening my mouth and speaking to Ox again. This was for her. I was going to have to get creative for her.

"If you're asking me to shoot this," I said. "No deal. I don't do needles."

"Nah, this ain't no shooting gallery," Ox said. "Just snort the stuff."

The choice I made next had to be the right one,

or else I risked doing something that I'd surely regret. Once again, I *thought* hard and quick.

"Cool," I said, "but before, I *did* want to ask you about that chick you had with you when we walked into the back earlier."

I caught Dennis's sideways glance out of the corner of my eye. A devious smile curled onto Ox's face.

"Which one you talkin' 'bout?" Ox asked.

"The blonde that was sitting next to you," I said.

"Aw yeah," Ox said, rubbing his hands together. "You want to freak off first. I got you."

Ox walked over to the stairwell at the intersection of the living room and front door.

"I can't get it up when I snort too much, either," he called back to me in the living room.

Ox looked up the stairwell and whistled shrilly. It cut through the constant, crawling bass of the music playing in the house.

"Delilah!" he called upstairs. "Delilah! Get your little ass down here!"

He walked back over to Dennis and me in the living room.

"Sorry, Dennis," he said. "You lookin' a little tore down today. I don't know if any of the girls are with that."

Ox chuckled, amusing himself, while Dennis and I shifted nervously, waiting to see what came next.

"How many girls y'all got up there?" I asked, with a nod up to the ceiling.

"Usually we keep five or six on hand," Ox said. "It's a school night. That means it's slow. We got Delilah, Kendra, and another one—Heather—working tonight though."

I lowered my eyes as he spoke with utter confidence. But he didn't know that I was getting a read on the operation *and* formulating a plan. The second girl, Kendra, was the one I saw in the living room when I first walked in. The unclear parts that remained were that I didn't know if the man that was with Kendra was still in the house, and I hadn't seen the third girl, Heather, yet. The careful footsteps above us continued, but there was no way to know how many people were up there.

"Where is *Delilah*?" I asked, with phony agitation.

"You know how these girls be," Ox said.

Delilah's delay presented an opportunity, albeit a risky one. These people were dangerous, but my hatred for them and their business screwed my courage to the post.

"She's taking forever," I said. "I need to use the bathroom."

"The toilet down here is broken," Ox said, "but if you gotta piss, you can just go ahead and piss in it."

"I don't have to piss," I said.

"For real?" Ox said, pushing air through his teeth. "You need to go on upstairs then. There's a bathroom right at the top of the steps."

"Okay."

I started for the stairs.

"Yo, Tolbert!" Ox said. "If you see Delilah after you take a dump, tell her it's time to stop makin' herself look pretty. Time to work."

I nodded, turned back around, and started for the stairs. The stairs were covered in carpet, making it difficult for anyone to hear me coming up. It was dark on the second floor. I could see the open door of the bathroom at the top of the landing and four additional rooms. One to the left of the bathroom was closed with a sliver of light coming from underneath its door. The girls' changing room maybe? Another room right across from that one was dark with its door wide open. I made it up to the landing and surveyed the rest of the floor.

At the end of a short hallway across from the bathroom, there were two more rooms facing each other, directly behind the stairwell. The room to the left had its door cracked open with no light on. Now, Mack was smart to search me for weapons. Yet he wasn't thorough enough, being inexperienced. He'd found my .38 because it was easy to find. What Mack didn't find was the folding knife I had taped to the inside of my thigh. I freed the knife from the tape, opened it, and held it blade out in my right hand. I stepped quietly to the last room on the right.

That door was also cracked, and there was light emitting from it. As I inched forward, I could hear the muffled voice of a male—Mack's voice. Because of the intervals of speech, it was clear that he was on the phone. I reached the door and cuffed the knife. I took a long, deep breath and after I had all the air I needed, I slowly opened the door. Mack was standing with his back to me, on the phone. He turned around, and all I saw were his inquisitive eyes. He reached for the back of his waistband but didn't have the time to do anything else. I shot the blade right into his gut before he had the chance to retrieve his weapon. The cell phone cracked on the floor and Mack doubled over. The weapon he reached for was my .38. I took it from his waistband, put it in my shoulder holster, and searched him for any other weapons. He was clean.

He writhed on the floor and his eyes filled with water as his hands covered the wound that shined with blood. Mack couldn't manage any words because of the shock. He stared up at me with fearful, newborn eyes, yet he didn't whine.

I picked up his cell phone and looked down at him on the floor. I covered the receiver.

"The Moon?" I asked.

Mack watched me with glossy orbs for eyes and coughed out a breath. Blood spewed out of his mouth, leaving his lips covered in a glossy mess of pinkish saliva.

I took the phone and put it to my ear.

"Hello?" I said.

Dial tone.

I searched through the phone's call log and there was nothing but unlisted, private calls. I looked down at Mack and the beige shag carpet underneath him was flooded with his blood. I hefted him to his feet, which was no easy task. He was built solidly and his lifelessness made him even heavier. I sat him upright on the king-size bed, against the headboard, in what looked to be the master bedroom of the house. I looked to the nightstand to the left of the bed and saw my cell phone. I retrieved it and slipped into my breast pocket.

"If there's anything else you can tell me about the Moon and his operation," I said, "say it now."

His final breaths came in shallow fits. He began to twitch. I liked Mack in some strange way. Here was a kid who seemingly had the world at his fingertips, thanks to football. He had his choice of several big-time college football scholarships, at least. But an injury derailed his dreams and led him here. Mack traded in one game for another, and ultimately it sealed his fate.

He closed his eyes and stopped breathing as I held him upright. He slumped over softly on the bed after I let go. I walked out of the room and quietly closed the door behind me. The light inside the room to the left of the stairwell was still on. It had to be where the girls were, but I wasn't going to go inside that room yet.

I closed the blade on my folding knife before

walking slowly down the steps. When I reached the living room, I saw Dennis sitting alone on the L-shaped couch. There was an open fear in his eyes when he looked up at me.

"Where's Ox?" I asked, in a low voice.

He nodded past me. "In the bathroom," Dennis said in a hushed manner. "He said he was gonna come looking for you after he was through."

"Stay here."

I walked out of the living room and toward the bathroom in the hallway between the front door and the kitchen. I opened the folding knife and exposed its blade again.

I gripped the bathroom's doorknob and took another deep breath. I pulled it open and there Ox was, urinating into the broken toilet. The image of him in front of the toilet reminded me of the work he did—streaming drugs and young girls to a broken town. My blood curdled, and though it was not my intention to kill when I first walked into the drug depot, my thoughts and aspirations were left behind. I was outside of myself.

Like his partner Mack, Ox didn't have enough time to react. I lunged instinctively, like an open-plains feline. I put the blade up to Ox's throat and bent his left arm behind his back crudely, creating an unnatural curve in the limb. He whimpered. I turned him, positioning him in front of the mirror over the sink.

"Listen to me," I said, with a wild and prejudice rage emanating out of me—my breath, spoiled, my pores, clogged with viciousness. I wanted to kill *this* man. I hadn't necessarily wanted to kill Mack. I had to do it, or he would have certainly killed me. I waited for Ox to give me a reason to end his life.

"Mack is dead upstairs. If you have anything to say about the Moon, now's your chance."

"Even if I tell you something, I'm dead."

"Tell me something I don't know, and I'll consider turning you in. Let the law have its say with you."

He bucked with his lower body and tried to swing

his right arm to free himself. I pressed the blade into his throat, to the point right before breaking skin.

I put my mouth right next to his left ear.

"How could you do this to these young girls?" I asked. "How could you suck the life out of them?"

He delivered his most taunting, evil smile. I watched it in the mirror as it goaded and dared me. I turned away from the mirror for his sake. The reality of the spot I was in reflected back at me, and I released the pressure on the blade by a few degrees.

"If you wanna kill me, go ahead and do it," he said. "Those girls up there don't mean a thing to me. I'm just mad that I'm in this spot because of some silly little girls. Not even women."

I slashed his throat from left to right and the sink was painted by a warm stream. I let go of him and he hit the bathroom floor with a thud. I closed the blade and put the knife in my pocket. I washed my hands of his blood, but couldn't look at myself in the mirror while doing so. My eyes stayed lowered as I scrubbed hard. I exited the bathroom and hurried into the living room. Dennis was in the same spot as when I left him, with the same expression on his face.

"Mack and Ox are gone," I said, feral breaths shooting out of my mouth. I could feel my chest expanding and receding. My stance was one of those masculine affectations: my back was arched and my fists were balled, even though the violence was finished.

"But we're not out of danger yet," I said. "There's one more room up there."

"Let's just get out of here, Pete," he said. "The front door is right there."

"No," I said, "the girls are in that room."

"So what?"

"Just wait here."

I hopped up the stairs without caution to the landing, where I exposed the .38 from my holster and pulled the hammer back. The light was still on in the room next to the upstairs bathroom. I burst into the room with my gun raised and found Delilah and Kendra lying on the bed, nodding off. There was a small circular mirror on the bed between them along with a rolled up dollar bill. Delilah spoke, her narrowed eyes making it impossible to know who the words were aimed at, but the words were gibberish anyway. I placed the gun in my waistband and went out into the hallway.

"Dennis!" I called downstairs.

He appeared at the foot of the stairwell, staring up wildly.

"Come here!" I said.

Dennis walked up the steps and joined me inside the room.

"They're high. I think on heroin," I said. "I need you to help me put some clothes on them."

"You're bringing them with us?"

"Yes. There should be another girl in here, Heather."

I scanned the room for Heather, along with items to clothe the girls. I found a pair of sweat pants.

"Here! Put this on her."

I threw the sweatpants to Dennis and nodded

to Delilah. When I walked to the opposite edge of the bed, I saw a pair of long, white legs. The body was in the seated position, leaning on the bed at a forty-five degree angle. I got closer. The girl wore a red wig, white bikini-top, white underwear, and white knee-high socks with red polka-dots. She was alive—the low murmur of her breathing could be heard—but not awake.

"Heather," I said in a low voice.

She did not move. I took the wig off her head and regarded her face. The girl's real hair color was brunette. Her body, lithe. The microscopic mole to right of her bottom lip gave it away.

"What the?" I said.

"Pete?" Dennis asked. "What's next?"

I didn't answer. He walked around to the other side of the bed and looked down at me with unblinking eyes.

"I got the one girl dressed, Pete," he said. "Should I dress the black one too?"

"I found her," I said, looking away from Dennis, keeping my eyes glued to Winona Daughtry.

"We gotta go, Pete."

That statement brought me back and I stood up, and again scanned the room. I found more articles of clothing and we quickly dressed Kendra and Winona.

"Here," I said. "Throw her over your shoulder."

He lifted Delilah, and I did the same with Kendra. We walked downstairs and out of the front door. It was about five o'clock, and luckily no one was outside to see us putting the two girls into my backseat. I ran back into the house and gently lifted Winona onto my shoulders. I placed her into the last space I had in my backseat and pulled away from the curb, leaving a little rubber on the road.

10

As I PULLED UP A FEW BLOCKS AWAY FROM THE
Note, the dusk was settling in. I put the car in
park and turned off the ignition. The three girls in
my back seat were still asleep. Dennis and I hadn't
exchanged a single word on the ride.

He looked over to me.

"You aced Mack *and* Ox?" he asked. "Damn.
That's some *Terminator* stuff. I'm gonna have to
leave town. The Moon is gonna kill my ass."

I reached into my back pocket and pulled out
my wallet. I took out all the bills and replaced my
wallet.

"The Moon will never know you were with me," I said. "I'll never tell another soul."

He sighed and shook his head.

"That ain't right," he said. "The video camera, remember?"

"Damn!"

"I have to get out of town."

"Here," I said, handing him the money. "That's a little over a hundred dollars. It's all I have on me. If you tell me where I can find you, I'll send you more."

"Nah, this is fine," he said, folding the cash and putting it in his front pocket.

"You should leave town," I said, "but you'll be able to come back soon. Like I said, let me know where you'll be, and I'll send word when it's safe to come back."

"What are you gonna do?" Dennis asked.

"I'm gonna deliver Winona to her parents and kill the Moon."

"I meant with the other two girls," he said, nodding to the back seat.

"Oh," I said, exiting my daze and entering something that resembled reality. "I'll take them to my place tonight and when they wake up, ask them about the Moon and his operation."

"You know you're crazy, Pete?" he said. "Do you know that?"

I smiled for some reason beyond me. "Here I am thinking all this around me is unusual and sick, and yet *I'm* the one being called crazy."

Dennis smiled, probably, at the irony of my statement and our entire day together. He reached for the handle on the passenger door.

"I'll most likely go to jail for killing Ox," I said shaking my head. "It's weird. I feel bad for killing Mack, but he was going for his weapon. I have no remorse over killing Ox."

"I don't want to hear no more about it, Pete," Dennis said.

"Okay," I said.

"These girls'll be scared, waking up in some place they've never been before. And if they're really junkies, they'll get dope sick real quick."

"Think they'll talk to me?"

"If you offer them money or drugs," he said. "But if they're addicts, I wouldn't believe a word they say."

"I believe you, Dennis," I said.

He looked me right in the eye for what felt like a full minute. There was no shame in his eyes even though his position in life as a drug addict brought on the judgement and sometimes hatred of his fellow citizens.

He extended his hand out to me and I shook it.

"You're a good dude, Pete," he said, with a smile. "Good, but crazy."

"I appreciate your help today, Dennis."

He opened the passenger door and put a foot on the concrete. He chuckled to himself before exiting.

"Whatchu gonna do to the Moon, again?" Dennis asked.

I looked straight ahead at the descending indigo all around. It was supposed to be a full moon that night, and damned if I didn't look past the street lined with cars and sweet-smelling Acacias, and tilt my vision up to see the big, bright shining thing up there. I didn't know what it meant at that moment for me to see the moon in all its naked glory, but it was pretty when it bounced off that kind of sad, blue sky.

"See you around, Pete."

He got out of the car, closed the door, and walked right past the Note. I don't know if he got high that night or any other night for that matter. I never saw Dennis again.

11

THE THREE GIRLS IN MY BACK SEAT WERE STILL fast asleep when I pulled up to Florence and Rick Daughtry's home. I lifted Winona out of the back seat and carried her to the front door. With no free hand, I kicked at the bottom of the door and waited for the footsteps.

"Yes?" Florence said before beholding the sight. She put both hands up to her mouth and then the tears came.

"May I?" I asked, nodding to the inside of the house.

Florence stepped aside and walked in. I placed

Winona on the couch in the living room, and Florence quickly covered her with a blanket. She turned to me and gave me a hug that meant more than a "thank you" for finding her lost child. There was a weight to the hug. Truth was, I wanted a hug too. And as much I as didn't want to let go, I knew I had to because there were still two girls in my backseat.

I pulled away slightly from Florence. "I have to go."

"Won't you stay for dinner? It's the least—"

"You all need to be together tonight. She could wake up at any time, and I want her to feel comfortable and safe when she does. I'll stop by tomorrow."

Florence nodded and turned her attention back to her sleeping child.

I turned to leave.

"Pete," she said. "Thanks."

I nodded and left the house, closing the door behind me.

Delilah and Kendra slept through the ride, as well as during the time I carried them—one by one—up to my apartment. Neither of them had any identification on their persons. With a closer look, I realized that they were, in fact, both very young—sixteen, eighteen years old, tops.

After getting them settled into my bed, I took a long shower. I was wiped out and didn't want to get out from under the cold flow of water. I wanted to *be* that water, free to move, free to fall away if I chose. After drying off and changing, I sat down on the couch in my living room with a cup of "relaxation" tea. It wasn't until then that the shock and pain of killing two men truly hit me. The possibility of murder was one of my reasons for quitting the force, and I knew I would have to live with killing Mack and Ox for the rest of my life. On top of that, the video camera above the door at the house in West Odessa would most likely send me to prison for a long time. Once the investigation for the killings of

Mack and Ox were underway, I expected a knock on my door. But for the moment I had time to think.

The way I saw it, this thing happening in Odessa, the exploitation of young girls, had to stop. I didn't understand it, and quite frankly it scared the hell out of me. I was willing to kill some more if it meant putting a stop to not only the Moon, but anyone else in Odessa who was taking advantage of young girls.

I had found Winona Daughtry and was relieved.

I wasn't satisfied, however. I recognized that satisfaction and relief were two separate and opposed things. I *could* have let it go right there and simply waited for the knock.

But it wasn't over and I had to know more.

I thought of phoning Jerry Calhoun and describing the events of my blood-soaked day, but then decided against it. I was simply too tired and would call Jerry in the morning. Besides, Jerry would be reaching out to me anyway if he had heard anything on the fringes of what I already knew about the Moon, or to give an old friend a heads-up on when the authorities would come knocking.

I settled into a cross between spastic intervals of uncomfortable sleep and wide-open lucidity. There were no sounds coming from my bedroom. The girls were still asleep and that was fine; I wasn't ready for any more heaviness before morning. I gave myself until the sun came up to be a private detective again.

When the first ray tiptoed into my living room window, I was wide awake. I checked on Delilah and Kendra, and though I wanted to wake them and start my work day, I let them sleep a while longer. My morning coffee helped me form a plan, a way of prognosticating my interactions with the girls when I got a chance to talk with them.

Finally, there was movement in my bedroom. I heard a rustling in the bed and then tentative foot-steps. The door to my room opened, and once again I heard steps toward the bathroom. The toilet flushed, and then either Delilah or Kendra paused outside the bathroom to wonder just where in the hell they were. The footsteps recommenced and got closer and closer until Delilah was standing in front of me in my kitchen.

"Hello Delilah," I said. "I have orange juice. Apple juice too. And I can also make some eggs. Oh, and there's coffee if you drink it."

She stared at me for a little while and, surprisingly, wasn't emotional or outwardly frightened. I didn't know what was going on inside Delilah, but perhaps putting up a wall was her way of showing emotion, namely fear.

I took the liberty of pouring her some OJ and handed her the glass. She accepted it and took a first sip while watching me over the glass. Her eyes were alert. I sat down at the kitchen table and opened up the front page of the latest *Odessa American,* which was delivered to my doorstep each morning. There was no mention of Mack and Ox's bodies being found at the brown house on the west side of Odessa. I put the paper down and took a sip of my coffee before looking over at Delilah again.

"I know this is strange," I said, "but I'm not going to hurt you. I didn't bring you here to hurt you or take advantage of you."

She stretched and then shuffled over to the table. She took the chair across from me.

"Then why did you bring me here?"

That was a difficult question to answer, beyond the simple reason of getting her and Kendra out of a bad situation. I wanted to help the two of them. I wanted to help all of the defenseless girls who were in their position. But I knew it wasn't possible. I also knew that these young girls were being failed in their homes long before they ended up in this state.

"I . . . " I said and stood up from the table. "I got you and Kendra out of that place."

"What do you mean?" she asked. "Me and Kenra stay over there with Ox."

I stared into my coffee cup.

"Ox loves me."

"Delilah," I said, "Ox . . . he doesn't love you."

Delilah stood up suddenly from the table now.

"Don't say that!" she spewed. "He does love me. Who are you? You don't know anything about it!"

I took a deep breath.

"This isn't easy," I said.

"What do you mean?" she said, her eyes beginning to well up. "Does Ox not want me anymore? Do I work for you now?"

"Oh no," I said. "No, no, no, Delilah. You have the wrong idea. I took you out of that place. You don't ever have to go there again. You don't *belong* to anyone."

She was confused, and that torrent of conflict within her stunted the tears in the corners of her eyes. Her face was peculiar because of this, a mix of befuddlement and sadness. Sadness, for what? I didn't understand it. But to her, those men in that house represented a concoction of emotions.

"I want to leave," she said.

"You can," I said, calmly. "You can leave whenever you'd like. But I just want to ask you a few questions before you do."

"Questions?" she asked, eyeing me contemptuously.

"Yes, and before I ask you anything, I want you to know who I am. I want to make it clear that I am not trying to fool you in any way."

"Okay."

"My name is Pete Hamilton, and I'm a private detective," I said.

"You're not a cop are you?"

Thinking about the way I dealt with Mack and Ox, I said, "Far from it."

"So what do you want from me?"

"What do you know about the Moon?"

"The Moon?" she said.

The look on her face was now one of astonishment, and I believed it. Delilah seemed to wear everything on her countenance.

"Yeah, you've heard of the Moon, haven't you?"

She shook her head with the same look of perplexity as when I posed the first question about the Moon.

"Okay. How about someone by the name of Johnny Five?"

At this, she scoffed and then laughed. "Mister, I don't know where you're getting these names from, but they're really weird. I don't know anyone who goes by those names."

"Do you attend Permian High?" I asked.

She laughed again, this time bitterly, showing teeth and tongue. "I stopped, um, attending anywhere a year ago," she said. "But when I did go to school, I went down in Midkiff."

Midkiff was a small oil town, about fifty miles southeast of Odessa. No connection to the Odessa-Midland operation the Moon had working.

"What are you doing up here?" I asked.

The smile was gone. She just shrugged and watched me.

"The Moon is a drug dealer," I said. "He's the one that Mack and Ox worked for."

"I don't know anything about that," she said.

"Know Les Myers?" I asked, grasping at a straw that was rapidly moving away from me.

She shook her head and sighed. Her glass of orange juice was sweating as it sat on the kitchen table between us. The day promised to be a humid affair. I put my head down to gather my thoughts. She showed no caginess when it came to answering my questions; she was sure, confident when she maintained that she didn't know the Moon or Johnny Five. I, on the other hand, was completely in the dark. The one surety I had believed from the start—that Johnny Five and the Moon were, in fact, the same person—was unfounded.

"I gotta be going now, mister," she said, standing up cautiously from the kitchen table.

"Okay," I said, looking down at my watch. "Go wake Kendra and we'll get on the road. It's gonna take a little while to get down to Midkiff with morning traffic."

12

AFTER DELILAH ROUSED KENDRA OUT OF BED, I
quickly changed. Kendra for her part, was even
more in the dark about the identities—shared or
otherwise—of Johnny Five and the Moon.

The Moon was disciplined enough not to mix
business with pleasure. I didn't ask Kendra any
questions aside from how she was doing. My only
condition for the two girls was that I would not drop
them off anywhere other than their parents' homes.
They objected to this at first, and I told them that
if they didn't want to be dropped off with family,

the Odessa police station on Grant Avenue would have to do.

I dropped Kendra off first because she lived in Pleasant Farms, and that was closer than Midkiff. It was strange at first, that the Moon brought girls from as far as Midkiff to work in Odessa. But on second thought, nothing was too strange for this case, and I wondered where else he brought girls in from. And though Kendra was not thrilled to go home, the woman who opened the door for her— her grandmother, I presumed—was moved to the point of tears. When it was Delilah's turn and we got on the road to Midkiff, she tried to talk me into dropping her somewhere else. I directly mentioned the police again and she got the point that I wasn't kidding. We pulled up to the address that she had given me. I parked in front of the one-story rancher and let the engine idle.

She stared out of her window at the house for a moment. There was something inside that repelled her. This place wasn't home for Delilah, but the address was safer than the brown house on the west side Odessa. This was all I could do. Delilah's parents had to do the rest.

"Come on, Delilah," I said. "I have somewhere to be."

"I'm gonna just get out again," she said. "Right after you leave."

"What you do after I leave is up to you," I said. "But just remember . . ."

I thought of the things I'd had to do the night before to save Delilah and Kendra from that house. Mack and Ox would not have let me take these two girls away from that place. I had to end their lives to do so. And here Delilah probably thought that I had negotiated their freedom with some financial arrangement.

"Never mind," I said, shaking my head.

"See you around, mister," she said.

"See you."

Delilah got out of the car and took the walk to her house. After a few knocks on the front door, a woman—a more weathered version of Delilah—opened up and stood in shock at the sight in front of her. The woman wrapped her arms around Delilah as if there was a grave mistake made in letting her go in the first place. The woman eyed my car as she hugged her daughter. The woman didn't know who I was, a friend or abuser. They walked inside the house together, and the woman shut the door behind them. For all she knew, I was one of the men who had possessed her daughter. None of that mattered though. Delilah was home now. Hopefully, she would stay there.

An anger burned in my gut after dropping Delilah off, and it caused me to drive like a maniac back to Odessa. Twice on the ride, I called Jerry and he didn't answer either time. I left a message on the second try for him to call me back.

13

I ASSUMED THAT FLORENCE AND RICK HAD TAKEN the day off to be there with Winona. Both of their cars were parked in the driveway when I pulled up to the house. I got out, walked to the door, and knocked twice. Florence opened the door with tears in her eyes yet again.

"She didn't escape, did she?" I blurted out involuntarily.

"No," she said, dabbing with a tissue. "I'm just happy."

"Happy is good."

"Please come in."

The house was lighter, greenhouse-like. The musty smell was gone too. It all made sense and even caused me to smile as I followed Florence through the living room and kitchen and onto the back patio where Rick was sitting with a cigarette and a cup of coffee. I reached out to offer him a hearty handshake.

"We'll never be able to repay you," he said, as he stood to greet me.

We shook.

"It's okay," I said.

"Would you like a coffee, Mr. Hamilton?" Florence asked.

"Please, call me Pete," I said. "I'm fine."

"I insist," she said. "Let me make you a cup of coffee."

I nodded. "Black."

Florence went back into back into the kitchen and returned quickly with a steaming mug of coffee. She placed it down in front of me on the patio table and sat in the seat adjacent to me, creating the same triangular configuration as the first time the three of us talked in person.

"Winona asleep?" I asked, before a warning sip of my coffee.

"Yes," Florence said. "As soon as you left yesterday, she woke up. And after I bathed her, we put her in her bed." Florence began to cry again and her tears were not redundant in any way; rather they were justified. This woman had lost her daughter, her only child, and through a set circumstances, that child was found. Florence was afforded a second chance to do it right and I hoped she would use that second chance wisely. The torrent of emotions inside her must've been immense. Hell, I wanted to cry too. But the job wasn't done yet. Maybe I'd have myself a cry after it was all over, perhaps from a prison cell.

"I'm sorry," she said. "I'm just a mess."

"Don't say that," I said. "You can cry. It's okay."

"Pete, tell us how much we owe," Rick chimed in from the other end of the table.

"Thank you, Rick, but I don't think now is the

time to talk about money. I'll send you an invoice. and we can settle up later."

Rick didn't reply. He leaned back in his chair and regarded me with something like admiration. When I was there a few days before, I couldn't wait to get out of the Daughtrys' presence. It was different this day. Even the weather turned an unexpected corner; for a late September day in west Texas, it was unseasonably cool and crisp. I closed my eyes and took in a lungful of air and let it burn my chest.

"You didn't question her or anything last night?" I asked.

"No," Florence said.

Rick shook his head.

"Good," I said.

We shared a pause.

"I'm gonna get these people," I said, unprompted.

Both parents' eyes expanded to the point of dilation.

"You've done enough," Florence said. "More than enough. We don't expect anything else from you.

We're thankful you came into our lives, and you'll always be special to us. But you don't need to do anything else."

There was a sound by the patio door, and I swung my head to see Winona. She was awake and looked fine. Normal. When I stood up, she walked over to me and gave me a hug, squeezing me tight. The strength and resolve of her grip surprised me. She finally let go, and the four of us sat down together.

Winona sat between her mother and me. She closed her eyes and let the cool breeze hit her face. I closed my eyes and did the same.

When the breeze died down, we both opened our eyes.

"Winona," I said. "If you don't mind, I'd like to ask you some questions. If you're not ready, I understand. We can talk whenever you're ready."

"I'm ready," she said, with a deep breath.

Florence exploded with another round of tears and shot up from the table. "I'm sorry," she gasped. "I can't."

She walked inside the house, and Rick stood up to follow her.

"Are you sure you don't want to hear this?" I asked him.

"It's hard for me to hear it too. I should go inside with her. And besides, we trust you, Pete."

I nodded.

Rick walked inside and closed the sliding door behind him. There was another cool breeze, and I waited for it to pass before starting up again.

"Who is the Moon, Winona?"

All she could do was nod as a tear streamed down the left side of her face.

"I'm sorry that I went through your journal, but I needed to find something to help me find you," I said. "The pages were almost all empty. There was no writing, anyway. I found the two sketches of the Moon on the last two pages."

"You know, yesterday when I was in that house?" she asked.

I nodded.

"I kept wishing that someone was going to come in and rescue me."

I watched her steadily; my eyes would not have blinked, even if I forced them to.

"And you did," she said.

That revelation was followed by a prolonged period of silence. There was no need to rush, so I didn't. And neither did she. After Winona finished another round of crying, I reached into my jacket pocket and took out the sketches. I handed them to her, but she simply put them face down on the patio table.

"What's with the mask?"

"I first met him at a Halloween party last year, and the white mask was a part of his costume. That party was strange all around, but the Moon, he relaxed me and made it okay. Not fun or anything like that. Just okay."

"Did he drug you?"

"He never forced me to take drugs," she said. "I wanted to take them. But he always provided them."

"Do you know his real name?"

"No," she said, shaking her head.

"Do you know about his operation?"

"You mean the drugs and girls?"

"Yes." Winona sighed as this meeting between us became heavier with each question. And part of me—a big part—wanted to stop asking, but I knew there could be one missing piece that could give me an advantage over the Moon, Jerry Calhoun, and anyone else associated with them that might emerge.

"Before I forget," I said, "you were abducted a little over a week ago, right? This didn't start out as you running off?"

She looked past me and into the house before speaking.

"I wasn't kidnapped," she said.

"So the Moon is someone you trusted?"

"Yes. At the beginning," she said. "He has this way of talking to you. It's like a fairy tale. One of those stories where the monster is really nice on the surface, but once you get too deep . . ."

Her eyes became surrogates for a faraway look.

"I don't understand, Winona," I said, leaning in. "What's special about him? How did he draw you in?"

"I had a crush on Les Myers for the longest time," she said. "But he would never even take me out. It wasn't until the Moon came into my life that Les changed toward me."

"How?"

"The Moon is close to a lot of Permian's players," she said. "They get drugs and girls from him. The players worship him, really."

"Were you one of the girls the Moon had working for him?" I asked.

She lowered her eyes. "For a little while," she said. "It got too crazy, and I stopped."

"Is that how you and Les got together?"

"At first. The Moon told Les how I could perform in bed and that changed Les's mind about me."

"You and Les had a relationship, then?"

"For a little while," she said. "But then . . . then I got pregnant."

"Was Les the father?"

She nodded. "He didn't believe me that it was his. He said that since I was sleeping with other guys, one of them must've been the father. But I swear, I wasn't. Les was the only one I was with at that time."

Her eyes filled up again as they watched me.

"I believe you," I said.

"I tried to give Les his space when I first got pregnant, and by that time, the Moon wasn't paying any attention to me. So I panicked. I started bothering Les about what we were going to do, asking him if we were going to keep the baby or not."

"What can you tell me about Johnny Five?" I asked.

Her expression changed to bewilderment.

"How do you know about that?" she asked.

"I went to Midland, Winona. That's the name you wrote for the emergency contact the day you had the procedure. For a while, I thought the Moon and Johnny Five were the same person. But now I'm not so sure."

"No," she said. "They're not the same person."

"So who is Johnny Five?" I asked.

Her ever-malleable expression turned to embarrassment now. The longer this went on, the more she spoke, the less sense it all made.

"Johnny Five is a nickname I made up for Les," she said.

"I don't follow."

"Les's middle name is John and he wears the number five. Get it?"

"Wait. Les wears number fifty. I saw him wearing it at practice the other day."

Winona rolled her eyes. "Fifty is his practice number. He wears five during the games."

My shoulders sunk and I sighed in frustration. How could I have known that Winona's interest in Les could've led to an odd mix of Les's middle-name *and* jersey number? The conflation was strange, so I didn't beat myself up about it too much. Luckily, the revelation was unimportant to the case, and not really a revelation at all, like most teenage fixations.

"And this is a nickname that's known inside of Permian?"

"No. I made it up. No one knows it."

I sighed again and shook my head.

"Why did you write that as your emergency contact?"

"Because I knew no one would've been able to trace it. And I don't know, writing it down on that form made me feel closer to Les in some way."

"Who was with you that day of your procedure?" I asked.

"The Moon."

"I thought you said the Moon had forgotten about you when you got pregnant?"

"He did. When I really started to pressure Les about the baby, Les lost it. He told his dad what happened and then his dad told Coach Freeman. A few days later at school, I was called down to Coach Freeman's office. I didn't know what to expect. I was so scared. When I walked in, Coach Freeman was in there with Les's dad. Les wasn't there. Coach Freeman told me that I could never talk to Les again and that it was over. After that, I felt alone. Like I had nowhere else to turn."

"Did Coach Freeman and Les's dad pressure you into having the procedure?" I asked.

"They said they didn't believe that it was Les's child. But I know they were lying because they told me that I had to get an abortion. Why would they tell me I had to get rid of the baby if they didn't think it was Les's?"

"You tell me."

"They said that the allegations would kill Les's scholarship offers. That even though it wasn't his child, being connected to *me* would hurt his football career."

"So the school sided with Les because of how much he means to the football team, and it led you back to working for the Moon?"

"Like I said, I was all alone. I couldn't tell my

parents. I couldn't tell my friends at school because then the rumors would start to fly. So I got in touch with the Moon, and at first he told me that he had no use for a girl once she got pregnant. But after a little while, I convinced him to loan me the money to get the abortion. He came with me because I had no one else."

"The Moon doesn't seem like the kind of person who changes his mind out of the goodness of his heart," I said, acridly. "Why the shift to being your support system?"

She dipped her head again.

"I promised him that I'd work off the money through, you know."

"The day you got the abortion, were you scared in any way?"

"Scared? No."

"Calm, then?"

"Before the procedure, the Moon gave me four Valiums to relax. So I was calm."

I leaned back in my chair and tried to process

everything. It was no use. I stood up and when I did so, the face-down sketches caught my eye.

"You're a good artist, aren't you?" I asked.

Winona's eyes lit up.

"How do you know?"

"Seeing your drawings made me think that, and when I talked to Courtney the other day, she confirmed it."

She smiled and blushed.

"Can you draw something for me?"

"Now?"

"Yes. I need you to draw me a sketch of the Moon's face. Without the mask, of course."

Winona thought about it, but it didn't take long. "Sure."

She got up from the table and walked inside. Ten minutes later, she reemerged with a large, note-pad-sized piece of paper, folded in half.

"Here," she said.

I took it and slipped it into my blazer pocket.

"Thank you."

Winona gave me another hug and we said our goodbyes. When I got into my car, I unfolded the piece of paper and regarded the sketch. It was detailed, and that fact, along with the speed in which she completed the drawing, was testament to her skills.

The Moon had stringy, dark hair and a ratty mustache. He was thin. There were craters left behind from his own pimpled adolescence. And the only feature of his face that called for a second look was the disturbing nature of his eyes.

14

AFTER TRYING TO FORCE MYSELF TO SLEEP THREE or four times, I gave up and dialed my friend in Fort Stockton. He never liked to sleep, and the reality of his current health situation made it difficult to sleep now. He was a cop down in Pecos County. One of the best and most trustworthy cops in the force, he had risen quickly as the leading detective in the violent crime unit. He *was* a cop. His new reality read early retirement; during a joint investigation with the U.S. Border Patrol, where a great deal of the work was done undercover, he had led the way on busting a steady caravan of women being brought across the border illegally to work the topless bars and backroom brothels in south Texas. The eight-month investigation rose and swelled to the point where a meaningful arrest was feasible.

He was not afraid to go after the cartels like so many of his border patrol colleagues, and while his commanding officers dragged their feet as they waited for word from above, my friend formulated a plan. Unwilling to wait for his bosses' permission, he set up a meeting with the investigation's primary target with the intention of turning the target into an informant against the cartels. This risk, this reckless throwing down of the gauntlet, came from somewhere in my friend's belly. That's what he told me in the hospital after the meeting with the target, anyway. You see, the meeting went awry, and the target opened fire on him. A bullet entered his right thigh and severed the femoral artery. My friend lost his leg; hence, the early retirement.

I let the phone ring because it took him a while to get to the phone now.

"Hello?" he answered gruffly.

"Hey," I said.

"Pete."

"I found Winona yesterday."

"I heard. Florence called me a little while ago. I was waiting for your call."

"How are you getting along?" I asked.

"Oh, it ain't as hard as it was at first, but I suppose there's some cruelty to that. It'll never be like it was."

"You know, I . . . " I paused to take a deep breath. "I think I'm about to do something reckless. I mean, I've already done some crazy things on this case, but I'm fitting to do it again."

"And you want me to talk you out of it?"

"I suppose. It may be too late though, like I said."

There was silence on the line.

"I guess it wouldn't stop me from doing it again anyway," I said.

My friend's gravelly laugh was familiar, and that detail caused me to laugh.

"Since your mind is already made up, I'll leave you

with this," he said. "Remember senior year? We were really fitting to have a good season, with me chasing the quarterback to high hell and you manning the back-end. That was a damn good defense."

"Yup."

"Well, you did something before the season started that solidified our friendship for the rest of our lives," he said. "We weren't really good friends before this thing happened, remember?"

"I remember."

"Here's this guy, Pete Hamilton, comes out of nowhere, this undersized guy, and starts on varsity for two seasons. And what he do? He quits the team because the coach is a wife-beater."

There was air between us again.

"When I found out that was why you quit, I said to myself, 'I like this crazy asshole,'" he said. "And that's where our friendship *started*. We share certain views on important things, right? Our mommas were both married to drunks who were loose with their hands. I know you think about that every day. I sure as hell do."

I pulled the receiver away from my mouth. The blood rushed upward again, just like when I was a child. My pulse quickened. My stomach quivered and gnawed on itself. The room felt like it was closing in on me. I put the receiver back up to my ear just to get some relief.

"Sleep well, Pete."

"You too."

We hung up and I went to bed. At first I was too restless to sleep, but exhaustion eventually prevailed and I slipped into a sleep of utter discomfort.

. . . .

I woke up in a sweat because in my haze the night before, I had forgotten to crack the window in my bedroom. It was Thursday and I decided not to make any moves. It wouldn't kill me to wait one day. There were no calls to make, no digging in anyone's past. Winona Daughtry was safe at home, and that afforded me the luxury of waiting one more day. That was, unless the Odessa Police Department kicked down my door and arrested me for murder.

I ate breakfast for what seemed like two hours.

With nothing to do, I waited by the phone in the kitchen. On one level, it made sense because I *was* waiting to hear from Jerry Calhoun. He'd inform me that the department had me for a couple of murders in West Odessa. I could count on Jerry for that.

As I waited, I set up a makeshift target at one end of my living room. The target was just a four-by-four piece of wood that I had cut out and attached to legs. I went to the other end of my living room, sat on the couch, and began throwing my folding-knife into the wood. Each time I threw it, I got up and pulled it out of the wood, and repeated. I had gotten good at this over the years, good enough to hit the same spot on the target during these practice sessions.

When the call or rapping at my door never came, I put the target away and folded the knife, replacing it in its sheath. I went into my room and retrieved a shoebox from underneath my bed. The shoebox held a 9mm semi-automatic pistol that held sixteen rounds. It was the same gun that the OPD issued its troops. I had found the gun reliable during my time in the academy, and after quitting, I purchased one for myself even though I had no shield.

Both of my guns—the .38 and 9mm—were checked, loaded, safetied, and put into my shoulder holster.

15

IT WAS THE DAY OF THE BIG GAME—LATE FRIDAY afternoon—and the lights were warming up over Ratliff Stadium. The whole town of Odessa buzzed for this early season matchup between Permian and Midland, two rivals. I was buzzing for a different set of reasons. I had no idea what I was getting myself into.

Whatever the situation, I was ready. Two guns were harnessed inside my shoulder holster under a suitably heavy blazer, considering the evening was cool, and thus my attire called no attention to itself. I also packed my folding knife, taping it once again to my thigh. I parked my car among the rest of the fans in Permian's massive parking lot surrounding the stadium. In attendance were young and old fans, joyous in their backing of their beloved MOJO. I filed into the stadium ahead of the lingering tailgaters, and took a seat in the bleachers, five rows up, fifty-yard line, behind Permian's bench.

The two teams warmed up, and with the help of the program I'd received at the front gate, I found out that Les Myers did, in fact, wear number five on game day. I shook my head.

As the players from both sides trickled onto the field, I tracked Les Myers when he emerged. He began his warmup by running through half-speed tackling drills with the rest of his linebacker mates. There was a definite intensity to Les Myers—something that college coaches salivated over. I peeled my eyes off Les long enough to watch Coach Freeman as he oversaw his entire outfit at midfield. He stood there confidently, as his team braced for a confrontation.

The bleachers started to fill in on both sides. I kept

an eye out for people around me who fit the physical description of the Moon. He was a sick human being from everything I had unearthed about him up to that point. I wouldn't have put it past him to be sitting near me in the bleachers while the action took place on the field. But there wasn't anyone in my section with shoulder-length brown hair.

Courtney Scott hadn't sent word of the after-party's location yet. She had said before that because of the cops, the location wouldn't be set until right before game. There were still fifteen minutes before kickoff.

"Permian High School would like to welcome everyone in the stands to this early season matchup between two of west Texas's best teams," the PA announcer bellowed. "The visiting Midland Bulldogs against your MOJO Panthers!"

The home team's fans erupted and then joined into a slow, rolling chant of "MO-JO! MO-JO!" that moved all around the stadium. Midland had a nice-sized cheering section behind its bench, but that number obviously paled in comparison to the swells of MOJO fans around Ratliff Stadium.

Midland won the toss and elected to receive the ball. There was a buzz from my cell phone inside of my breast pocket. The text from Courtney came through with the party's location and code word "cuando" that would secure my entrance. I knew the neighborhood of the party's address. It was in Odessa, close to the Midland line. I thanked her and told her not to go to the party, without any more details. She took a couple a minutes to respond, but when she did she confirmed that she wouldn't be at the party.

"Come on, son! Get off that phone!" a man next to me said in a warm drawl. "It's game time!"

"Oh yeah," I said, putting my phone away. "It's hard to get away from work."

This was serious business, the game between Permian and Midland. Not only were bragging rights and early season playoff positioning on the line, but also the right to personal freedom. I was not allowed to be on the phone while these kids did battle on the field. The diehards had their own code for the behavior and etiquette that constituted a fan. I was an outsider.

The ball was kicked into the west Texas night, and Midland ran it out to midfield. When Les Myers led Permian's defense onto the field, a quick look at the size disparity between the two teams forecasted a long night for Permian.

I was wrong.

Les was a force on Midland's opening drive of the game. On first down, he knifed into the backfield and stopped Midland's running back for a loss of two. The next play brought a sack, also by Les, who used a well-timed blitz right up the middle. Myers capped the drive with an interception on third down, which he ran back to the end zone.

It was seven to nothing, Permian, due to the play of Les Myers. The "MO-JO!" chant crested again in earnest.

Midland took possession again and fared no better

than it had on its first drive. Les was once again a thorn in the rival school's side, with another pair of tackles and a near second interception on third down. I couldn't help but think of Winona Daughtry as Les displayed his brilliance on the field. In most peoples' minds around Odessa, Les's play justified some minor discretions off the field. That's not to say that most people would be okay with local football players being involved with pimps and drug dealers, who drugged and sexually exploited girls, but Les wasn't guilty of those things. And although I did not agree with his actions toward Winona, I knew that he was a young man and not as deserving of blame as the much older and more experienced. They were the ones who okayed this behavior by enabling it, or at the very least, turning a blind eye to it.

I understood it—it was all about making Les feel untouchable on and off the field. If Les was made to feel like a God in the halls of Permian and on the streets on Odessa, he had no other choice but to go out onto the field to take what was rightly his. To dominate. To destroy. And perhaps, as an unintended consequence, to exploit. We were all guilty, really. Everyone in the stands was complicit.

Permian led twenty-one to three at halftime. The MOJO marching band came onto the field to stimulate Permian's fans before the blowout could commence in the second half. I left my seat to walk around the stadium during halftime.

I stopped at a concession stand to buy a soda and out of the corner of my eye, I saw a man. Tall, thin, long brown hair, ratty mustache. Face acne-scarred. It registered as quickly as it might for a computer that the Moon was standing about twenty feet away from me—in another concessions line. He wore a black hoodie and blue jeans. The only difference between the picture Winona drew and the man standing near me was that his stringy hair was tied up in a ponytail rather than at his shoulders. I took my eyes away; I backed out of the line and went to the back of the line that the Moon now headed.

I took out my cell phone and dialed Jerry.

"Hello?"

"Jerry!" I said, with movement all around. The marching band on the field muffled the sounds of people scurrying around for refreshments and the restroom.

"Pete?" Jerry asked. "Where are you?"

"At the game."

"I didn't know you followed Permian. I couldn't make it to the game tonight. I wish you would've told me. Had I known, I would've gotten out of the thing."

"I'm staring at the Moon, Pete."

There was a thoughtful pause on Jerry's end.

"Jerry?"

"Yeah."

"How fast can you get here?"

"Ah, Pete. I'm tied up here. It'll take a little while."

The Moon was finished at the head of the concessions line. He turned around holding a soda in one hand, popcorn and candy in the other.

"I gotta go, Jerry. I'll text you soon!"

I hung up and caught up with the Moon. I kept a healthy distance between us. After staying in pursuit for ten steps or so, the Moon stopped in his tracks, causing me to do the same. He turned around and looked upward, eyes moving up into his skull, as if he had forgotten something at the concessions line. His hoodie read *MOJO* in big, white block letters. After he finished his thinking, he headed right toward me. I turned quickly and ducked behind a family of four, pulling the son in front of me.

"Excuse me!" the mother said.

"Just relax," I said.

I let go of the son's arm and tried to use him for cover. The Moon's eyes flashed as he passed by, and he quickened his step. I hustled not to fall too far behind, but by this point, it was crowded in the concessions area. I weaved through and around groups of people in an effort to keep up. After almost tripping over a young Permian fan, and almost falling down face-first as a result, I looked up and could not find the Moon.

I started running in the direction that he was walking, but he was nowhere to be found. I looked all around me; everyone there seemed to blend together into one mass of black and white.

"Damn," I said.

There was nothing to do but continue in that direction. If he changed directions, I surely would've seen. I reached a part of the concessions area that opened to the field. I turned and looked into the corridor that led to the stands. A ponytail was walking away from me and into the corridor. I sprinted to catch up.

"Hey!" I shouted.

The Moon turned around and smiled before going on his way. The end of the corridor opened up and there was a logjam of fans trying to either go up or down to their seats. The Moon was somewhere in that crowd. The third quarter action was just starting up on the field. The horde swayed and spit me out on the end closest to the field. I looked down in the stands near the opening. He was not there. I looked up the stands, right above the opening. Same.

I turned and looked back into the throng of fans. The Moon was standing at the front of the mass, grinning like the sadist he was, wagging his finger at me. I was too far away to grab him, so I reached into my blazer pocket and took out my cell phone. I snapped a picture of him as fast as I could and hoped that it would be in focus.

The Moon turned around and forced his way back into the crowd. I followed, but after squeezing back into the concessions area, he was gone for good.

I checked the picture and it was in focus—the Moon was smiling in the snap that would help send him to prison. There was no need to continue chasing after him. I had him. He had no idea that I'd be at the after-party.

I texted the address of the after-party to Jerry.

He replied that he'd be there.

The pw to get inside is CUANDO, I texted.

Ok, he replied.

The Moon'll be there, I texted.

There was no response from Jerry. I texted the Moon's picture to him. I wanted my almost-partner to know who he was looking for when he got to the party.

Thnx, Jerry replied after a few minutes, finishing our exchange.

Instead of going back to my seat for the second half, I watched from a spot near the track in the east end zone. Permian hit a long pass early in the third quarter, a fifty-yarder that set the Panthers up at Midland's two-yard line. The home team punched it into the end zone on the next play, making the score twenty-eight to three.

The stands were filled with MOJO fans that wanted blood. The masses wanted Midland to surrender, to admit defeat. The entire Lone Star state needed to be warned about how good Permian was, and future challengers would need to take heed of this brutal lesson being taught by the Panthers. The outcome of the game was a formality. Permian had pulled its best players by the end of the third quarter. It was almost time to party.

I looked up to the scoreboard and took a deep breath. Odessa would never be the same after tonight. I knew it, the Moon knew it, but the rest of the people in the stadium had no idea. People felt safe in their communal love of Permian, of football. And as I looked around the field one last time, I felt the slightest urge to walk away. To *not* take this away from them.

It had to be done though.

By the time I walked to my car, the game was over. I sat and watched the people as they got into their cars and left the stadium. Thirty minutes later, my car was the only one left in the vast space. I drove closer to the school and parked near the locker room exit. Players were starting to come out and either meet up with family members for rides or hop into cars of their own. No Les Myers yet. And no sight of the Moon either. I kept my eyes peeled for

Jerry as well, but that seemed like more of long-shot. He'd hopefully be at the party-house on the Odessa-Midland line.

More players began to exit out of the locker room. I refocused and saw Les walking with a couple of his teammates. They approached a luxury SUV, of which Les was apparently the owner. They lingered for a moment before getting in the truck and pulling away from school. I gave them a fifteen-second head start before I started my engine.

16

COURTNEY'S PARTY LOCATION WAS ACCURATE. I didn't have to follow Les to the party, but he led me there anyway. I parked a couple of streets over from the party-house and walked over to it. I didn't see Jerry's car parked anywhere near the house, nor did I see any police cruisers.

The house itself was nothing special—a modest, two-story rambler. This wasn't your normal high school party either. Usually, the streets neighboring the party-house are filled with cars and lingering packs of inebriated teenagers. This was more of an exclusive affair.

I knocked on the door, and after a minute, a young woman answered. She poked her head outside.

"What's the password?"

"*Cuando*."

She opened up and stepped aside.

I walked into the foyer.

"Where's the bathroom?" I asked her.

"Right there," she said, pointing to a half-open door to the right of where we stood.

"Drank too much beer at the game," I said.

She shrugged and rejoined the party.

I went into the bathroom, locked the door, and turned on the light. I splashed water onto my face before clicking off the safety on my 9mm and loading a bullet into the chamber. I slipped the gun into my waistband. I readied my .38 as well before replacing it in my shoulder holster.

When I got out of the bathroom, I entered into what I thought was the living room through a cascading curtain made of beads. On this side of the beads, the space was wide open. No couches or coffee table. I scanned the scene and it was strange, much more restrained than the high school parties I remembered going to. The light was low and the music was as well—trance-like. The guests were a mix of young and old and everyone looked to be relaxed and confident in this improvised dance room. No one outwardly exhibited that they were under the influence. I didn't see any girls who looked like sex workers. The females that were there seemed to want to be there. I turned and saw Les Myers out of the corner of my eye. He was leaving the living room with the same teammates he left Ratliff Stadium with. I followed them out until they reached a doorway that led to a set of descending stairs. The basement, I presumed.

They took the stairs down.

When I reached the basement, it became clear that this was where the real party was happening. There were three large couches set up in the room, along with a full bar. There weren't any drugs in plain view, but I did smell marijuana smoke.

I looked around for the Moon.

Three young women exited through a door in the corner of the basement. The door seemed to lead to a changing room. The women strode with confidence over to Les and his teammates and sat on one of the couches in the opposite corner of the room. They wore nothing but bikinis and thigh-high heels. One of the Permian players took out a cigarette filled with marijuana and put a light to it. He took a puff and passed it to Les.

I walked over to the couch and joined them.

Les was confident in his repose. He took two long pulls off the cigarette before passing it along. He leaned back on the couch and put both hands behind his head. He exhaled. His sureness on the field carried over to his real life.

I crowded the group's space.

"Excuse me," Les said. "Do you mind?"

I looked him in the eyes and then pulled out the .38.

"We're gonna have to talk, Les," I said.

The girls screamed and bolted into the changing room. Les's teammates recoiled in horror.

"Drop the weapon, Pete," a voice came from behind.

I knew the voice and the wave of nausea within my gut returned.

I turned around.

"I said drop the weapon," Jerry Calhoun repeated.

I turned and watched Jerry as he stood in the doorway of the basement, pointing his departmental nine at me. The Moon stood next to him, wearing the same outfit from the game, black 'MOJO' hoodie, blue jeans. His eyes were severe, like in Winona's quick-sketch. A brooding scumbag.

"I'm not gonna do that, Jerry," I said, with my revolver raised at the pair now.

"You're a real moron, Pete," Jerry said, with vitriol in his voice. "First you quit the force and now you're making waves, all over some young hooker."

I pointed the gun at the Moon.

"I'm glad to see you," I said.

"Same to you, Pete," the Moon said.

"What's going on here, Jerry?" I asked. "How are you mixed up in all this?"

"The night before we were supposed to be sworn in, you called me, Pete," Jerry said. "Remember what you told me?"

I nodded. "I told you that the idea of being a cop didn't feel right anymore. I told you that it's impossible to be a good cop because the bosses are always bad."

"That's right," Jerry said. "I took it that you were too soft to wear the shield. You would've been good. Don't get me wrong. Investigation comes natural to you. But you're not tough enough."

I readied my empty hand.

The Moon reached behind his back but he was too slow. I drilled him right in the chest with a shot from my 9mm. The Moon stumbled back into the doorway and hit the bottom stair with a thud. Jerry unloaded and I jumped over one of the couches and crouched behind it. Les and his teammates did the same right next to me. The silence filled the space. Paint from the ceiling flecked down onto us. Gun smoke caused Les and his teammates to cough.

Jerry took two steps into the basement and then stopped.

"Stand up, Pete," Jerry called.

I looked over to Les and his teammates. I held up a hand and mouthed, "Stay down."

"What did the Moon have on you, Jerry?" I yelled. I peeked up over the couch and Jerry let one go. I ducked back down.

"You have no play here, Pete," he said.

I looked over to Les again. He wasn't so calm now. The protection had been stripped away. He was just a child.

"Let the kids get out of here, Jerry," I yelled. "I'll give myself up if you let these kids leave."

Jerry stood still and that made me think he was considering my offer.

"Throw your weapons over the couch," he said. "Then I'll let them go."

I safetied both the .38 and 9mm and dropped them on the other side of the couch. They hit the faux-wood floor and rattled to stillness. I freed my folding knife from the tape around my thigh.

"Okay, Jerry," I said. "Let them go. That was the deal."

"You guys stand up!" Jerry said to the football players.

Les and his two teammates stood up cautiously. One of the players had wet his pants.

"Beat it!" Jerry said.

When Les neared Jerry, he put a hand to the linebacker's chest. Les's two teammates were long gone.

"Remember, Les, this guy behind the couch is the bad guy. You saw him shoot first. I'm the cop, apprehending the bad guy. Just remember that."

Les nodded and darted out of the basement and up the stairs.

"Let's do this, Pete," Jerry said. "Stand up."

The knife's blade was exposed. I gripped it to be

thrown, just like in my living room. It would be a blind throw. I tried to envision where Jerry would be standing in relation to couch.

"You have until the count of three, Pete."

I closed my eyes and took a deep breath.

"One."

The knife shook in my right hand.

"Two."

I steadied the knife and my grip on it.

"Three."

I stood up and in one motion, threw the knife at the large body that was three big steps away from the couch. The blade struck Jerry right in the heart, and he collapsed to the basement floor with a clunk. He shot a few rounds into the ceiling on the way down, but the impact of the fall knocked the gun loose from his hand. Jerry lay on the basement floor at the feet of the Moon, who was also on his back, fighting for air.

Jerry knew he couldn't take the knife out of his chest because it would only hasten the end. His only hope would be talking me into calling for medical assistance. I picked up my guns and holstered the .38.

The Moon was almost finished. Even then, he held a sadistic grin on his face that was a menace to humanity. I put a bullet in his head from my 9mm to finish the job.

Jerry struggled now and looked up at me with big, wondrous eyes. His beached frame took up what seemed like a lot of the basement floor.

I crouched down close to his face.

"Why'd you do it?" I asked. "Why would you get mixed up with this scumbag?"

Jerry swallowed some blood that was simultaneously rising and falling through his throat.

I looked down at my old friend. I didn't shoot him. Jerry would die shortly after I walked out of the basement.

17

I CALLED COACH FREEMAN AT HIS HOME RIGHT after leaving the party-house. I told him that he had to meet me in his office at Permian High and gave him an hour to do so. He resisted my overture at first. But there was something in my voice, I guess, when I repeated my demand.

He agreed to meet.

I went home to change clothes, and as I put on a fresh pair of socks, the TV in my bedroom was tuned to the local news. The anchor broke the story of the murders at the rambler on the Odessa-Midland line.

I turned off the TV before leaving my house to meet Coach Freeman.

While driving over to Permian, I thought about the sleepy streets of Odessa, which would be rocked with the scandalous announcements that were about to come. The only thing that needed to be resolved now was how the news was to be broken. I had my view of it, and the rest depended on Coach Freeman.

The parking lot in front of Permian High School was completely empty, it being the wee hours of Saturday morning. The Friday night spectacle was over and it was time for the city to recover. I walked into the school and through the halls. Coach Freeman said that the locker room door would be open for me and it was. I walked into his office to find him sitting at his desk.

"Hamilton," he said upon laying eyes on me.

I walked over to his desk and sat down in front of him. We eyed each other. I'm sure with his competitive nature, he tried sizing me up. But he had no idea what I had just been through, and besides, I was an open book.

"What is it that you want?" he asked.

"I want you, Les Myers, Floyd Myers, and Permian's administration to be investigated for forcing Winona Daughtry to have an abortion."

Coach Freeman leaned back in his chair and, surprisingly, he didn't try to bully me. He simply watched me.

"You know, a man like you who walks in here and talks to me like this," he said, "must have some kind of high card."

"Something like that," I said.

"What if I say no?"

"I'm gonna go to the papers and spill everything that I've uncovered. And I'm not coming here to you now so that certain people can be spared. This isn't a bargaining session," I said.

He continued watching me.

"No one gets out squeaky clean. Not Les. Not

you. Not anyone at this school who knew about Les and Winona's relationship and her pregnancy," I said.

He took a deep breath.

"I don't get out clean either," I said.

Confusion took control of Coach Freeman's stare now.

"I have some things that I have to live with too," I said.

Coach Freeman leaned forward, and it was clear that he realized we had reached the point of no return.

"Okay," he said. "The way you came in here and tried to talk to me about Les told me something about you. I knew right then you were as stubborn as a mule. There was a look in your eye, like none of this scares you. And then when I saw you up there watching our practice, I knew we were in for trouble."

I stood up from Coach Freeman's desk.

"What do we do next?" he asked.

"I'll be in Monday morning to talk to you and

Principal Martinez," I said. "I'll tell you everything I found out then."

Coach Freeman laughed nervously. "Are you sure I can't give you something to think about over the weekend? To change your mind?"

I shook my head and left the office.

I got in my car and drove by the Daughtrys' house. All was silent, with both Florence and Rick's cars parked in the driveway. I didn't stop for long.

My apartment was the most inviting that it's ever been. I collapsed onto my bed and didn't leave it for the rest of the weekend. Monday would be a big day, a heavy day, so I deserved the rest. The Winona Daughtry case had taught me a lot. I just knew it. It was simply too soon to apply what I had learned.